MISSION MUMBAI

MAHTAB NARSIMHAN

MISSION MUMBAI

A NOVEL OF SACRED COWS, SNAKES, AND STOLEN TOILETS

SCHOLASTIC PRESS / NEW YORK

Library of Congress Cataloging-in-Publication Data

Narsimhan, Mahtab, author.
    Mission Mumbai : a novel of sacred cows, snakes, and stolen toilets / by Mahtab Narsimhan.—First edition.
        pages cm
    Summary: Dylan, an aspiring photographer, is spending a month in Mumbai with his friend Rohit Lal and his family, but knowing nothing of Indian culture, he cannot seem to do anything right (do not hit cows!)—and the situation is made worse by the tensions within the Lal family over whether Rohit should be raised in India, which Mr. Lal's wealthy sister is pushing for.
    ISBN 978-0-545-74651-9
1. Culture shock—Juvenile fiction. 2. Manners and customs—Juvenile fiction. 3. Friendship—Juvenile fiction. 4. Families—India—Mumbai—Juvenile fiction. 5. India—Social life and customs—Juvenile fiction. 6. Mumbai (India)—Juvenile fiction. [1. Culture shock—Fiction. 2. Manners and customs—Fiction. 3. Friendship—Fiction. 4. Family life—India—Mumbai—Fiction. 5. India—Social life and customs—Fiction. 6. Mumbai (India)—Fiction. 7. India—Fiction. 8. Humorous stories.] I. Title.
    PZ7.N1634Mi 2016
    [Fic]—dc23

                                                                            2015024673

10 9 8 7 6 5 4 3 2 1   16 17 18 19 20

Printed in the U.S.A.   23
First edition, April 2016

Book design by Carol Ly

FOR RAHUL, AFTAB, AND COBY

ONE

I WANTED A CLEAR SHOT BUT THERE WERE TOO MANY people blocking the way. Clutching a weapon that was highly inadequate for this dangerous mission, I crept toward the beast. It sat still, its crazy eyes glaring at me. I lunged forward and attacked.

The stick landed on the cow's backside with a loud whump. She jumped up with a plaintive moo and bolted, udders swinging, crap bombs exploding in her wake. The stench mingled with the smell of rotting garbage in the midday heat, making my eyes water. I ignored it all, my Nikon camera whirring, capturing close-ups of the animal.

People scattered as she ran. The road was *almost* usable now. That is, if you avoided the puddles of poop. I got some pictures and cleared the road—mission accomplished! I looked around, waiting for a congratulatory thump on my back. Rohit's flat (*not* apartment as he kept correcting me) in the heart of Mumbai was just a few steps away at the elbow of the L-shaped lane. I glanced at the second-floor window, hoping Rohit had seen my heroic stunt, but he was nowhere in sight. Even though

I was older (and wiser) by a good four months, his mom had made him promise he'd keep an eye on me during my very first trip to India. I'd tried to explain to her that it was the other way around—*I* was Sam taking care of Frodo in the *Lord of the Rings* of life. All I got for my efforts was a pat on my back and a "We shall see, *Beta*," from Mrs. Lal.

An ominous hum filled the air. I whirled around. A rapidly swelling crowd started gathering, screaming stuff I didn't understand. Angry faces moved closer, pointing at me and glaring. The whiff of stale food, sweat, and cow dung assaulted my nose. My blood turned icy even though my scalp was hot enough to fry an egg. What was *wrong* with these people? I'd moved the cow so they could use the road and they were mad at me? It *must* be the weather. No one could stay sane in ninety-eight-degree heat without an air conditioner and a cold can of root beer.

Rohit still hadn't made an appearance. "Good people," I pleaded, folding my hands in a *namaste*. "I come in peace. What's the problem?"

They shuffled even closer, continuing to stare at me. Sweat trickled down my back. The cow plunked down in the middle of the road and mooed. It had the effect of a war cry. The mob charged.

I barreled through a weak spot in their defense, for once glad I was so big. I pushed aside a skinny boy who tried to grab me, and hurtled toward the safety of Rohit's flat—my home for the next three weeks. If I survived the next *three minutes.*

"Rohit, HELP!" I screamed as I raced up the steps to the second floor, my camera clutched tight in my slick hands. I was so loud my parents in New York could have heard me. Feet pounded up the stairs behind me as I thumped on the door and jammed my finger onto the doorbell. Rohit's flat had one of those weird deadbolt locks that needed a key, and I hadn't bothered carrying one. The door flew open just as a swarthy man reached the landing below.

"STOP!" he called out.

In your dreams. I pushed Rohit aside, jumped in, and slammed the door shut. Trembling, I sucked in a lungful of cumin-scented air. Somewhere in my panicked brain it registered: Mrs. Lal was making lunch and it was going to be another gastronomic adventure.

"Open up!" said a gruff voice from the other side of the door. Thoughts of food evaporated.

"What's going on?" asked Rohit. He pushed his glasses up his long nose and peered through the keyhole.

"You gotta save me, Ro, my bro. These people have lost their marbles."

"Dylan, what happened?" asked Mrs. Lal as she stepped out of the kitchen, wiping her hands on a towel.

"Er . . . you see, there was this ugly Warg monster on the road, like the one Bilbo rescued Thorin from in *The Hobbit* and—" Rohit was shaking his head imperceptibly and I stopped. Mrs. Lal liked facts. She wasn't high up on the imagination scale.

"Dylan, speak," said Mrs. Lal, snapping her fingers. "That man is going to break down my door if we do not open up soon." She was a small woman with a large voice. Even Mr. Lal avoided arguing with her.

"There was a cow in the middle of the lane," I blurted out. "Traffic was going around it. I felt sorry for them."

"Oh no," said Rohit, his elbows jerking inward. It was this really weird tic he had, and he looked like he was about to do the Chicken Dance around the flat. "Tell me you *didn't*."

"Yeah . . . I tried to move it." I looked from son to mother, omitting the minor detail that I'd also wanted some good action shots.

"*Hey, Ram,*" said Mrs. Lal, smacking her forehead with her palm. "This is going to be very, *very* bad. Rohit, didn't I *tell* you to keep an eye on him? You *never* listen to me."

She glared at him. Rohit glared at me. I had no one beside me so I glared at the wicker sofa. The pounding on the door was deafening. It sounded like a million angry people out there and only a flimsy door was between us.

"How did you move the cow?" said Mrs. Lal, flinging the towel away and tucking the edge of her saree into her waist. Battle stance. Those men better watch out. My money was on Mrs. Lal.

"I hit it with a stick," I said.

"Tell me this is a joke," said Rohit, his eyes goggling behind his glasses.

"No," I squeaked. "Just a little tap on the backside and now these weirdos are out for my blood. What did I do wrong?"

"You have a *criminal* inside," the gruff voice called out. "Give him to us."

"Take Dylan to the bedroom and do *not* show your faces till I call you," Mrs. Lal said. "Go. Now."

Rohit grabbed my arm and dragged me off just as his mom opened the door. The landing was boiling with people and my heart quivered like Jell-O. Mrs. Lal stood tall, all four and a half feet of her, barring the way.

I peeked out the bedroom window, gauging the distance to the ground in case the mob overpowered Rohit's mom and I had to jump. We'd just gotten to India and I was already in trouble. Mom's words echoed in my mind.

"Dylan, remember you're their guest. Please behave yourself."

I stared into her brown eyes, knowing exactly what she was trying to say: Be respectful, don't let your imagination run wild, and don't overeat. She knew how carried away I could get with all things fantasy—mostly books and movies—and good food.

"I'll try my best, Mom," I said.

She smiled and patted me on the back. She was British and rarely gave in to any PDA. "I know you will."

"I suggest you also think about what I told you, young man," Dad said. *"I expect you to join a soccer team in the fall. And if Rohit has a gym at his place, use it regularly. You can get a head start on the season by losing a few pounds."*

"That's enough, Neil," Mom snapped. *"Your son is going to have a good time with his friend. Can you let him enjoy his trip, and lecture him later?"*

"You spoil him, Rosemary. Just look at him—all he wants to do is eat and take pictures all day. What kind of future does he have?"

"So why don't you step up and help?" Mom replied, her voice shrill with emotion. *"Oh wait. It's because Mr. Hotshot Moore has time for everyone in the world but his family!"*

And that's when I left, their angry voices following me all the way up to my room on the second floor of our massive brownstone.

The door to Rohit's flat banged shut, bringing me back to reality. Mrs. Lal called out, "Dylan, Rohit, come here, please."

My heart stopped galloping. I wouldn't have to jump out the window after all. I swiped my sleeve across my sweaty face and stepped out of the tiny bedroom.

"Yes, Mrs. Lal."

"What is it, Ma?"

Her face was a thundercloud. *"Do not hit any animals on the road ever again.* Most of them, *especially* the cow, are sacred in India. Hindus worship cows. Am I making myself very clear?"

That explained the heightened emotions among the popu-lace. I put on an I'm-very-sorry look.

"When you hit a cow, it is as if you're slapping one of their mothers. It is considered a huge insult."

"But Mrs. Lal, it . . . she, er . . . their mother was sitting in the middle of the road churning out crap by the cartload, and obstructing traffic. I was only trying to help."

"Cows have right-of-way in India," she said in a tight voice. "I explained to them that you did not know. Now, if *Rohit* had been caught hitting a cow . . ." Her voice trailed off, horror etched on her face as she gazed into the distance. Within moments that penetrating gaze was back on us. "I thought I told you to keep an eye on Dylan, *henh*, Rohit? This is the *first* time he's visiting India and you let him *hit a cow*?"

The shrill whistle of the pressure cooker shattered the omi-nous silence. We played pass-on-the-glare again.

"Sorry, Ma," said Rohit. His glasses slid to the end of his sweaty, shiny nose. He flicked the edge of the frames with a finger and they shot back up again.

"Sorry, Mrs. Lal," I echoed. "Won't happen again. I'll be very good to all animals from now on."

"Keep an eye on your friend," she told Rohit, wagging a finger under his nose. "If he gets into any more trouble, *you're* going to be in hot water. You used to listen to me but three years in the States have made you Mr. Know-It-All. I have lots to do before your cousin's wedding and I don't have time to babysit twelve-year-olds. At your age, your father and I—"

"I know, Ma, *I know*," said Rohit, his voice getting squeaky and high-pitched, which happened when he was stressed or angry.

She retrieved the towel from the floor, slapped it onto her shoulder, and walked into the kitchen. I flopped down on the sofa and stared at the fan. It rotated, sluggishly trying to push the thick, hot air around the room. It didn't make a difference—it was hotter than ever.

"That was crazy!" I said. "I'm sorry I got you in trouble."

"You could have been hurt." He sounded mad and a little scared. "You're *banned* from solo trips. From now on, wherever we go, we go together."

"Like Frodo and Sam," I said, winking. "Cool."

"It's not funny, Dylan," said Rohit. "If anything had happened to you . . ." His voice trailed away and his twitch intensified. "I'd never be able to forgive myself."

"Lighten up, Ro. No way a cow-obsessed mob could hurt me. But honestly, you *were* supposed to be watching from the window, so it's just as much your fault."

Rohit opened his mouth and shut it again. That part was true. If he'd warned me, I wouldn't have *touched* the sacred Mother, let alone whacked her with a stick.

Delicious smells filled the flat, making my mouth water. Back home I'd been over to Rohit's place often enough to know his mom was a great cook. Now that I wasn't going to be torn limb from limb, I realized how hungry I was. I couldn't wait till lunch. But there was still so much to see and do. This was my first, possibly last, visit to Mumbai. I couldn't see my parents ever coming here. Not after what was probably happening back home. I refused to dwell on it or I'd be depressed for the rest of the day.

"Let's go for a walk," I said. "We have three weeks to explore this place and we're sitting here arguing. Besides, gotta get some exercise so I have more room for lunch." Rohit stared at me, twitching as if he were trying to pull up his shorts with his elbows. I've always been the one dragging Ro around.

A scrawny guy with skin the color of milk chocolate stood next to our teacher, Mr. Tintpulver, surveying the class with an almost defiant gaze. But his nervous twitches and tics were drawing whispers and sniggers from the class. I knew exactly how that felt. I'd gone through the same thing when I'd been the new kid. The bullies would only move on when someone newer showed up. I felt sorry for the guy. The next few weeks were going to be torture for him.

"Dylan Moore!" Mr. Tintpulver's voice brought me back to reality.

"Yes, sir?" I replied, thinking, Crap, crap, triple crap. Why me?

"I'd like you to be Rohit's guide for the next two weeks. Show him around, introduce him to your classmates, and make him feel welcome. Okay?"

"Sure," I muttered. There was no point arguing with Mr. T. He was old, but strict and stubborn. And super smart, but he'd slipped up this time. Pairing the twitchy new kid with the most unpopular nerd in class was social suicide for both of us.

Turned out that it was the best idea Mr. T ever had. Ro and I found out we had a lot in common—similar interests and pet peeves. We both loved to read, hated team sports, and didn't have brothers or sisters. I wanted to know more about India and what life outside of America was like, and Rohit was an expert. He wanted to fast-track integrating into the American culture and lifestyle, and I was happy to help.

At one point I'd said, "You know, this reminds me of one of my favorite friendships of all time—"

"Frodo and Sam in Lord of the Rings," *Rohit had cut in.*

I'd stared at him in silence. At last, a kindred spirit who loved Tolkien and—I'd come to find out later—all things fantasy. And who needed a friend just as much as I did. Ro and I had been best friends ever since.

"We're going out, Ma," Rohit said, popping his head into the kitchen. He jammed his feet into his shoes without bothering to untie the laces. "Listen," he said, his voice dropping to a whisper, "please don't get me into any more trouble. Ma is already stressed about having to face all our relatives here without Papa. I just want to get through this trip and go back without having her blow up at me twenty times a day."

"So what? She calms down just as quickly," I said. "You just need to know how to handle her better."

"When *you* do something stupid, I'm the one who gets yelled at," said Rohit.

"Me?" I said in mock horror. "I'm mostly awesome except when adventure calls. And this place is like an exotic movie location. How can you hold me back at a time like this?"

"Oh yeah?" said Rohit. "A hundred bucks says you won't make it to the end of our trip in this *exotic location*. You'll be screaming to go home in a week!"

"You're on, bro! Keep your money ready."

He punched me on the arm. I punched him back and got ready to grab him. Ro was such a lightweight that most times he toppled over with the lightest of taps from me.

"I'm used to winning," he said.

"So'm I."

"Lunch will be ready in an hour," Mrs. Lal called out from the kitchen. "Rohit, keep *both eyes* on Dylan. I promised Rosemary I'd keep her child safe."

I rolled mine as I grabbed my camera and an apple from the fruit bowl. Mother *and* son were overreacting. What trouble could a street-smart New Yorker get into in Mumbai?

TWO

WE STEPPED OUT OF THE BUILDING AND INTO BRIL-
liant sunshine. Sweat blossomed from every pore as
hundreds of UV arrows zinged their way into my skin.
Another few days and I'd be as brown as Rohit. *Awesome*. At
least then I wouldn't look like a huge piece of raw fish, and
maybe people would stop staring at me or deliberately bumping into me on the road.

The narrow lane bustled with life. Vendors pushed hand-
carts piled high with shiny steel vessels, men on cycles and
scooters wove between pedestrians, and women hurried
along, each with a kid or four in tow. The ancient buildings on
either side of the narrow lane, with their peeling gray paint
and barred windows, seemed like they would have a lot to
say, if only they could talk. The sacred Mother had moved
to a shady spot under a coconut palm at the end of the lane.
We ignored each other.

The smells of rotting garbage, spicy curry, and gasoline
fumes filled the air. It took some getting used to, but now it
didn't bother me as much.

Rohit pushed his glasses up his nose. "I'll show you Marine Drive by the sea, but don't expect too much."

"Anything with water sounds awesome, bro," I said. "I'm melting."

Rohit was quiet as he expertly navigated the trash-littered sidewalk.

"Don't you have poop-and-scoop laws here?" I asked. "That's an awful lot of dog poop."

"What makes you think it's *only* dog poop?" he said.

I tried hard not to think of how it got there, but now that Rohit had enlightened me, it was *all* I could think about.

We walked out of the lane and onto the main road, which was so packed with cars it could easily have been mistaken for a parking lot. Each driver was intent on out-honking the others and within seconds my ears were ringing.

"Why are they honking?" I asked. "There's no room to move."

"It's a habit," said Rohit, shrugging. "Do you *really* want to go? It's not what you're used to—my place or Mumbai. We could chill in a coffee shop till lunchtime." He refused to meet my eyes as he spoke.

"Are you kidding?" I said, nudging him along. "Let's explore. Don't you want to see what's changed since you were here three years ago? And I told you I need some exercise."

"No, I really don't care," Rohit said glumly and started walking. "And I thought the only thing you like to exercise is your mouth."

"Ha-ha."

I kept both eyes on the sidewalk as I followed him. Around me, Mumbai shimmered in the heat, the cacophony filling my ears, smells clogging my nose. It was the most populated city in India, with 12.5 million people crammed in 233 square miles of land, according to Wikipedia. This place was so cool and Rohit was dumb not to see that.

"Man, they're loud," I muttered as a taxi inched past, its driver draped over the steering wheel, horn blaring nonstop.

"You stay here long enough, you won't even notice it," said Rohit.

At the end of the main road was a long flight of stairs leading to a walkway high above the traffic. I jogged up the stairs, dodging beggars, stray cats, and pedestrians going down. My heart was pounding so hard with the exertion, I opened my mouth to take a deep breath and inhaled a fly. Ack. I coughed till it shot back out, unharmed.

At the top of the steps I stopped to catch my breath. Dad probably had a *tiny* point about getting more exercise. The thing was, with my large build, I *looked* athletic. But ask me to run a lap around a field and I'd be wheezing like a geezer.

A hint of salt wafted toward me on a lukewarm breeze. "I love this place," I said, snapping pictures like crazy.

"It's okay, I guess," Rohit said in a cool voice. "It's somehow dirtier compared to New York. And there are so many more people . . ."

I stared at him. "You need thicker glasses, Ro. New York is awesome, but this is different, so . . . so exciting. Can't you feel it? Even walking on the sidewalk is fraught with danger," I said, laughing. "You never know what you'll step into!"

"Don't make fun of Mumbai," said Rohit, jamming his fists into his pockets. "I warned you it's not up to your fancy lifestyle back home."

"I'm *joking*," I said, noticing his pinched mouth. "Why d'you have to be so serious?"

Rohit shrugged. "Just don't, okay?"

I didn't want to get into a fight, so I shut my mouth. Rohit was the best friend anyone could ever ask for but he could be so sensitive. We raced down the stairs on the other side of the walkway and through a narrow alley that reeked of pee. The walls of the buildings were stained with splotches of bright-red stuff, and some of it had puddled on the road. Blood was *everywhere*. My stomach churned.

"Gang war?" I asked. "Don't they clean up after . . . the murders?"

"You'll get to see the massacre soon. You can't leave Mumbai without seeing it at least a dozen times. Stay close," he said, his voice dropping to a whisper. I wondered if he was serious or if his dry sense of humor had finally arrived from New York.

"Okay," I said, my stomach gurgling with anxiety even as I snapped a few pictures of the blood-spattered walls. How could he talk about murder so casually? I'd come to know a lot about Rohit these past few years, but obviously there was a lot more to learn. I was going to pump him for details. I'd never seen a *single murder* back home, but from the sound of it, Ro was a pro. Cool.

A couple of shady-looking characters sauntered past, giving me the evil eye. One of them whipped out his cell phone, came right up to me, and took a picture. Hadn't they ever seen an American before? Apparently not, because they were still staring at me. I drew myself up, channeling the Dark Lords Sauron and Voldemort, and glared at them.

"Jaldi!" I barked, remembering a word from the last Bollywood movie I'd seen, which I thought meant "go away."

They laughed.

I hurried to catch up with Rohit. "What did I just say?"

"Fast," he replied with a smirk. "Stick to English, okay?"

"How do you say—'go away'?"

"Jao."

"Got it."

We'd reached another main road. Cars zoomed past, spewing fumes and adding to the haze and heat. Beyond this chaos was the Arabian Sea.

"There it is: Marine Drive," said Rohit. "Nothing much to see, really."

We ran across the road at the pedestrian crossing with at least a dozen other people. Heat waves rose from funny three-sided concrete stones that looked like giant Legos. They lined the wall along the parapet, shining wetly. Rohit identified them as tetrapods, placed there to strengthen the shoreline. At the far end of the curving sidewalk stood two buildings—one tall, one short—windows winking in the sun.

"Are those apartments?" I stood on the parapet for a better look. A light breeze came off the water, cooling me. It felt *so good*.

"The Oberoi hotels, a five-star hotel chain and hangout for the rich and famous," said Rohit in a flat voice. "I've been there a couple of times—it's fancy and very expensive. I can ask Ma to take us there if you want."

"*No. Way.* I've had enough of five-star hotels. I want to experience the *real* India. Small local restaurants, roadside vendors, home-cooked food is even better! Also, Mom's paid a load of cash for all my vaccinations. Might as well see if they work."

Rohit didn't answer but I knew exactly what he was thinking. My family was rich and it bothered him. I wanted to tell him that I would have traded my life for his, to have parents who paid attention to me for once, but I knew he wasn't in the mood for a lecture. Not after Mrs. Lal had given him one. Instead, I clicked a picture of a seagull diving into the water with the Oberoi hotels in the background, hoping it would turn out as good as it looked in real life.

"What's with all these pictures all of a sudden?" asked Rohit. "I didn't see you go nuts with photography back home."

"Is there anything you're passionate about besides food?" Dad said. His voice was low but there was an edge to it. He was in a bad mood.

I glanced at Mom. She'd caught it, too. The fragrance of a well-cooked pot roast filled the air. I wanted to eat, not argue.

"I love photography," I said. "That's why I've been asking for all this equipment on my birthdays."

"How will that improve your life?" Dad asked. "You're young and you need to be healthy. Like me. I bet I could outswim you. We could go to the pool right now and I'll prove it to you."

"I'm not unhealthy, Dad," I said, trying not to snap.

"Here's an idea . . ." he started to say.

Unfortunately I'd heard that idea before . . . only a few hundred times.

"Why don't you take up soccer? I could give you a few tips. After all, I was varsity captain, and it paid for my college education."

"Dad, you know I hate soccer! I love photography and you asked me what I'm passionate about."

"That's not really what I meant," Dad grumbled.

"Neil, he's going to India next week," Mom said. "Can you leave him alone for now? We'll discuss this . . . and other things when he gets back."

Dad stood up. "We're not done talking about this, Dylan. No son of mine is going to waste time and money on useless things."

Mom drained her almost-full glass of wine. I shoveled a fork-ful of pot roast into my mouth, looking anywhere but at him. Dad sighed and walked away.

"Earth to Dylan, come in, please," Rohit bellowed in my ear.

"If Earth doesn't shut up, he's going to be taking a swim, fully clothed," I managed to say calmly. I was desperate to talk to Rohit about Mom and Dad and the increasingly bitter fights they were having but somehow I kept putting it off. If I didn't talk about it, maybe it would go away. I knew I was being a baby but I wasn't ready to deal with it yet. I hurried to change the topic. "Speaking of swimming, is there a beach around here? A couple of laps in the water will help me work up an appetite."

Rohit grimaced and pointed. "Chowpatty's that way. You seriously want to go? The water's not clean. No one swims there and in fact I haven't seen anyone paddle in it, either."

"If Frodo had been this negative, he'd never have left the Shire," I said. A quick paddle in the water was just what I needed to cool off. Rohit, too, by the look of it. "I want some pictures, so come on already."

"Why? You still haven't answered my question."

"Later. Come on, race you to the beach."

"In this heat? No thanks."

"Party pooper," I said.

"Loser," he replied and turned in the direction of the beach.

Without company, sprinting was no fun. I walked, making a mental note to get some exercise in later. The sidewalk ended abruptly and we stepped onto sand.

A stray dog trotted up to me. Immediately I dropped to my knees and folded my hands in a *namaste*. I'd show these guys that even though I was a foreigner, I could follow customs and traditions. I wasn't going to make the same mistake twice!

Rohit grabbed a fistful of my T-shirt and yanked me to my feet. Not easy for someone a third my size and weight.

"Wha—"

"Stand up, you idiot," said Rohit. "People are laughing at us. *What* are you doing?" His face was red and I knew it wasn't just the heat.

"Your mom said all animals were sacred so I'm paying my respects."

"Not stray *dogs*," said Rohit. "You could get bitten and end up with rabies."

As if on cue, the dog bared its rotting yellow teeth, saliva oozing from the corners of its mouth. Flies buzzed around a festering sore on its shoulder. Laughter from passersby ringing in my ears, we hurried on, just a hair short of galloping.

"Only cows, okay?" said Rohit. "Also the king cobra, but only if it's been defanged or you'll die a painful death in under a minute. You could include squirrels, too," he said, warming to the subject, "but only the ones with three stripes on their backs. They're supposed to have been blessed by Lord Rama for helping him build a bridge to rescue his wife. But you can safely ignore buffaloes, monkeys, and pigs, and never touch dogs, cats, or rats unless you want rabies. Got it?"

I sorted out the menagerie in my head, the holy from the unholy, while screaming crows circled overhead as if mocking me, too. Vendors in colorful carts lined one side of the beach, which had a fair bit of debris lying around on the sand. It was *absolutely empty*. We'd be lucky to find a towel-size bit of free space on a hot day at Coney Island or Long Beach. Waves crashed to shore and I couldn't wait to get in.

"Wow, Ro, look at it. We have the beach all to ourselves. Doesn't anyone in Mumbai like to swim? Last one in is a loser!"

"No, Dylan, *wait*," yelled Rohit. "Don't . . ."

But I refused to listen to his negative comments again. I was hot and the water had to be cooler. A little trash wasn't going to stop me. I kicked off my sandals, wrapped my camera and Rolex (Dad would kill me if I ruined it!) in my T-shirt, and raced to the water's edge. I heard Rohit yelling at me to stop, but I ignored him. For once, I'd be able to tease him for being second.

I waded in to my knees, scooped up some water, and slapped it on my face. And immediately gagged. Something that had *no business* being in the water was now in my mouth—a wad of soggy paper that looked disturbingly familiar. I coughed and it shot back out into the water and sailed away. I looked down. My pale legs were pockmarked with bits of brown goo. Riding

21

on an incoming wave were plastic bags, seaweed, rags, and more brown blobs. My nose told me exactly what they were. I shot out of the water at warp speed. Frodo was going to be pummeled to pulp and Sam wouldn't come to his rescue—because Sam would be doing the pummeling.

Rohit was sitting on the sidewalk, shoulders heaving, laughing so hard he was crying.

"How . . . how could you not warn me?" I demanded, scooping up handfuls of sand and rubbing my legs with it, trying to take shallow breaths. I shoved my camera and watch at him, still wrapped in my T-shirt. "Don't drop them."

"Welcome to Chowpatty Beach," he gasped, flicking his glasses and hitching his shorts, looking like a shortsighted duck flapping his wings. "People . . . um . . . have a habit of throwing things in the water and some of the homeless use it as an outdoor toilet. No one swims here. I *did* tell you to stop."

I had nothing. All I wanted to do was go back to the flat and shower. For once no one bumped into me on the sidewalk and even the stray dogs gave me a wide berth. I galloped home as if chased by the ghostly Ringwraiths.

THREE

ROHIT'S MOM TOOK ONE SNIFF AS I WALKED IN
and pointed to the bathroom. I was shutting the door
when I heard her admonish Rohit. *Again*.

"Did you not tell him that the water is polluted with raw
sewage? If he's swallowed any . . ."

"Ma, I *tried* but he didn't listen," said Rohit. "He's fine so
stop yelling at me! A little water won't kill him."

The water wouldn't but what was in it might. I couldn't wait
to scrub my mouth with soap and brush my teeth.

"I can't be his babysitter all the time," Rohit continued in a
pained voice. "He has to use common sense some—"

The rest of it was cut off as soon as I shut the door but the
annoyance in Rohit's voice was unmistakable. I knew he hated
being told off, especially in front of an audience. And this was
the *second* time today.

*Note to Self: Don't alienate your main ally out here. Listen to
Rohit—at least once a day if possible.*

Lunch was amazing. I figured that since I had run up the
steps at Marine Drive and on the beach, I'd burned enough

calories for seconds. Maybe even a third if you counted the race back to the flat. I helped myself to *dal*, rice, chicken curry, and cottage cheese with spinach. Mrs. Lal looked pleased. As long as I worked in some exercise daily, I'd be fine.

I downloaded the pictures I'd taken in the last couple of days onto my laptop. They weren't too bad. The background was a bit blurry on a couple of the Marine Drive shots and in some the composition sucked. I'd gotten a good shot of the cow's profile but her eyes weren't visible. That would have really rocked the picture.

I wondered what my idol, Ari Valokuva, a Finnish photographer who'd settled in New York, would have done. He was world-famous and his picture *Solitude*—a lioness standing on a rocky outcrop, silhouetted against a fiery sunset—had been nominated best wildlife photograph of the year. And hours of trekking and waiting in barren lands for The Picture meant he was super fit, too. One day, with hard work and some luck, I could be as good as he was. I'd love to see Dad try to find something wrong with Ari.

• • • • • •

After lunch Mrs. Lal announced we were going to visit Rohit's *bua*. For a second I had visions of a large boa constrictor dressed in a saree, strangling me to death by way of greeting, or giving me a poisoned kiss on the cheek with a forked tongue. Noticing my puzzled expression, Rohit explained that *bua* was the Hindi word for "father's sister."

Even though Mr. Lal was arriving from New York a few days later, his sister couldn't *wait* to see us and had *insisted* we meet her right away. Mrs. Lal's announcement was met with a lot of eye-rolling on Rohit's part as he has mimicked his bua. Mrs. Lal quickly glared at Ro and fluttered around, visibly nervous. What was up with them? And just how scary was this boa lady?

"Are we taking the bus?" I asked as we walked out of the lane to the main road. I'd seen red double-decker buses rumble past, BEST written on their sides. The buses had no doors and people jumped on and off while they were still in motion. I'd caught a glimpse of a ticket collector standing by the door as one inched past. He wore faded khakis and a short-sleeved shirt, clacking a metal tong against a box slung around his shoulder as he handed out tickets. I was fascinated and wanted to snap some close-ups. This place was rife with great photo ops!

"No way," said Rohit, shaking his head vigorously. "I'm not traveling by bus."

"Why not?" Mrs. Lal and I asked in unison.

"Too crowded," he said. "We won't get a seat this time of day. If we're going to be crawling in traffic, might as well do it sitting down." His eyes had a steely look that his mom and I both recognized—he wouldn't budge on this. I had to admit, though, his logic was irrefutable.

"All right, we'll take a cab," Mrs. Lal said in a pained voice. "Living in the States has really spoiled you, Rohit. You used to love traveling by bus. You'd race to the deck and grab the seat right in front. And now just look at you!"

Rohit rolled his eyes, sneaking a glance at me. I knew why he was doing this. I wanted to smack some sense into him and tell him to stop trying to impress me, and stop feeling ashamed to take public transportation. So what if I had a car and driver at my disposal in New York? We weren't there now and I would happily have taken the bus for the adventure of it, and the pictures.

"Ma, that was years ago," Rohit said. "I'm sure Dylan would prefer a cab to a smelly bus. *Right?*" It was a question, but the accompanying glare made it very clear there was no argument.

"If they're called BEST, there must be something special to them," I said.

Rohit snorted.

"BEST is short for Brihanmumbai Electric Supply and Transport," Mrs. Lal explained. "The local bus can be a bit uncomfortable, but you decide, Dylan. You're our guest."

I didn't want to take sides between my friend and his mom. I wished Mr. Lal would get here soon so I could stop getting caught in the middle.

"I'm fine with either," I said.

"Traitor," Rohit muttered under his breath.

"Idiot," I replied softly.

"So, what's your aunt like?" I asked as we walked.

"Okay," he said, his tone implying the opposite.

Now I really wanted to meet this boa character. We'd been smothered by friends, relatives, and old neighbors of the Lals since we'd landed in Mumbai. No one called first—they just came. I'd already met tons of Rohit's cousins, aunts, uncles, and one pregnant relative even introduced me to her baby bump. I also met his cousin Nisha, the bride-to-be, who was beautiful. I couldn't say the same about her husband-to-be, Sanjay, who looked like he'd escaped from the ape house at the zoo. Every Lal was super nice.

Back home, *everyone* called before they came over. I saw my extended family maybe twice a year and even then the parties ended with hurt feelings, tears, and sometimes fistfights. I sighed, wondering if my moronic friend would *ever* figure out just how lucky he was.

We ended up hailing a black-and-yellow cab, its driver honking furiously just so he could crawl an inch ahead of the car beside him. It was not air-conditioned, but since the wait for another could have taken forever, we decided to take it anyway.

Our sauna on wheels shot away from the curb, narrowly missing a vendor with a basket of fruit balanced on her head. She cursed the driver loudly, shaking a fist at him. Rohit had taught me a few curse words, so I knew what she was saying. The cabbie gave it right back to her while Mrs. Lal tried to shush him, her eyes darting to me. I smiled, pretending not to know what was going on.

Pedestrians wove through the slow-moving traffic, not waiting for the light to cross. It was total chaos and I *loved* it. My life in New York was so predictable, and this mess was so exciting! It was almost like starring in my own Bollywood adventure.

The cabbie imitated a NASCAR driver while we swayed and jerked in the backseat. We slowed to pass a cow sitting in the middle of the road causing a colossal traffic jam. Cars and buses flowed to its left and right but not a soul dared to move it. The seriousness of what I'd done earlier came back to me and I was even more grateful to Mrs. Lal for saving the day.

Rohit poked me, his eyes sparkling. "Dylan, wouldn't you like to move that cow? You'll have the grateful thanks of every driver on this road."

"I wouldn't *dream* of touching your revered er . . . *other* Mother," I said, glancing at Mrs. Lal. "She looks comfortable where she is and we will let her be." I did a *namaste* as our cab crawled past. Rohit smiled as he punched my shoulder lightly, and I punched back, relieved his bad mood was evaporating.

Traffic crawled like a caterpillar on sleep meds.

"Shall I take inside road, madam?" the driver asked. "Marine Drive very busy now."

Mrs. Lal murmured her assent and the driver made a few twists and turns, taking us deeper into the heart of Mumbai.

Smog blotted out the sun while we marinated in the humid air tinged with gasoline fumes and the smell of rotten vegetables. Rohit pointed out that we were passing Crawford Market, the largest fruit and vegetable market in Mumbai.

In spite of the intense heat, there was constant movement everywhere. Men with long, narrow boxes on their heads ran alongside the cab, outrunning the slow traffic. Rohit pointed them out, explaining that they were *dabbawallas* who carried tiffin lunches to the white-collar workers of Mumbai from the workers' homes. They were so unique that case studies had been done on them at Harvard and they had a Six Sigma certification for accuracy. I was suitably impressed and took a ton of photographs from the crawling cab.

Crippled beggars sailed past on platforms fitted with wheels; cooks sat on the sidewalks frying a variety of foods in large woks, swiping at their sweaty faces with filthy rags. Everywhere I looked, cars and people jammed the streets. I kept snapping pictures, hoping my hand was steady enough. This would make a sweet collection.

Rohit sat back and closed his eyes, yawning widely.

"This place is awesome, Ro. Why don't you visit more often?"

He peeled a sweaty leg off from the black plastic seat, making a sucking sound. "For this?" he said, pointing at the glistening wet patch. "Give me New York any day. At least all the cabs there are air-conditioned and we don't have to wait forever for one."

I peeled my leg off the seat, too. It sounded like a wet squeegee on a windshield. I did it again and again, but stopped when I saw Mrs. Lal's expression.

"Sorry," I muttered.

She nodded absently, wrapping the end of her dupatta around her finger, which had turned white. Why was she so on edge? Because of Boa? How horrible *was* this woman? I couldn't wait to meet her.

"How much longer before we get there?" said Rohit, exhaling audibly. "I'm melting!"

"New York is hot, too," said Mrs. Lal. "Please stop whining, *Beta*. Dylan is handling it better than you."

That thoughtless comparison earned us both a glare from Rohit. I caught the driver smirking at us from the rearview mirror and glared at him. His smile vanished.

Mrs. Lal turned to me. "If you hadn't come with us, Dylan, Rohit wouldn't want to be here for his cousin's wedding."

"Thank you for inviting me," I said. "It's been fun so far. Right, Ro?"

Rohit took off his glasses and mopped his face with a tissue. "I've seen it all. What's the point in seeing it again? I'd rather explore the rest of America."

"You haven't seen your family in three years," said Mrs. Lal sternly. "And I haven't seen your manners since we landed in Mumbai. I suggest you behave yourself if you know what's good for you."

Rohit gave me another dirty look and I shrugged apologetically. Mrs. Lal stared out the window. She wore large sunglasses, so I couldn't see her eyes, but her mouth, drooping at the corners, gave her away. I wanted to say something to lighten the mood, but decided to keep my mouth shut. Most of the time I just ended up with my foot in it. I'd spent a lot of time at Rohit's in the last few months—sometimes for school projects but mostly because I wanted to get away from home. He'd sensed it but hadn't made me talk about it, and I really appreciated that. Now it was my turn to have his back without asking questions.

The cab dropped us at Colaba Causeway, in front of a building with fading yellow paint. Clotheslines decorated every balcony. I guess people here weren't embarrassed to hang up their underwear in public. I saw a neon-pink bra, a pair of granny panties, and everything in between. Mrs. Lal ushered us into the cool, dark building. The temperature immediately dropped to bearable. Facing me was an accordion-type metal gate.

"What's this?" I asked. "No wait! Don't tell me, it's the elevator!"

"Bravo," said Rohit gravely. "You should take a picture." He winked. The jerk was *enjoying* my reaction but trying not to show it.

I noticed more blood splatters on the walls by the elevator door. I pointed, wordlessly looking from mother to son. Evidently someone had been murdered here very recently, but neither of them seemed to care. They must have nerves of steel.

Rohit shook his head, looking worried. "More bloodshed. A word of caution—they don't like foreigners here. *Especially*

Americans," he added, his voice dropping to an ominous whisper. "You better be careful and always watch your back."

A cold finger traced a path down my spine. How could Rohit's aunt live in such a dangerous place without any kind of security or police protection? This was insane! "Maybe we should go home and call Boa instead," I said.

"What *nonsense*, Rohit. This is—" Mrs. Lal started to say.

"Ma, let's go," Rohit cut in as he jabbed the grimy elevator button. "You know Bua *hates* to be kept waiting." There was a loud groan and squeal somewhere above our heads.

"Er . . . maybe we should take the stairs?" I said. "You know, get the heart pumping, blood flowing. *I* sure could use the exercise." The elevator sounded like it was in the final stages of machine cancer. I had no intention of getting on it and ending my life quite so soon.

Mrs. Lal patted me on the back absently. "Not to worry. This was installed during the British Raj. It will still be going up and down long after we're all dead."

Not very reassuring at all. "Crap," I muttered under my breath.

"The building's only got fifteen floors," said Rohit. "Even if the elevator crashes it won't be fatal. You might lose an arm or leg at the most."

I gulped and wiped my damp hands on my shorts. The ancient elevator came to a stop with a thud. A tiny man in black pants and a black shirt slid open the accordion door. He waited patiently while we stepped into a space that made an airplane bathroom seem massive. It reeked of stale food and the mirrored walls offered multiple angles of my terrified expression.

"Maybe I'll take the stairs—" I started to say again but it was too late.

Tiny guy slammed the accordion gate shut and plunked himself down on the wooden stool that took up more space than necessary and had the rest of us standing on one another's toes. "What floor?" he droned in a bored tone.

"Fifth," said Mrs. Lal.

Fifth wasn't too bad. People had survived falls higher than that. I was going to be okay. I exhaled softly. Then inhaled. *Big Mistake.* I was right behind the elevator dude and the sickly sweet perfume of his hair oil crawled up my nose. I held my breath as the elevator slid past the floors in slow motion.

"Rohit, remember your manners and greet Bua properly," Mrs. Lal said, dabbing her forehead with her dupatta. "Or she'll say we've become snobs since we moved to the States. She'll complain to your father, and then I'll never hear the end of it. And Dylan, you be . . . just be polite and respectful," she said. "Okay?"

I nodded, still taking shallow breaths, praying I would live to see thirteen. Thankfully the elevator didn't plummet to the basement as I'd expected, and we stepped out into a dark corridor on the fifth floor. A lone bulb clinging to a cobweb-encrusted wire emitted a faint light that created huge shadows.

It reminded me of the time Frodo and Sam had followed the dwarf Gimli into the dark and dangerous Mines of Moria. It came as no surprise that Boa should reside here, given that she'd already stressed out my best bud and his mom though they had yet to meet up on this trip.

Something skittered past and disappeared into the gloom before I could make out what it was. I was glad I hadn't shrieked out loud, though my heart was pumping extra hard. We reached a plain white door and rang the doorbell. A wizened man opened the door, releasing a cool blast of air. Boa had an air conditioner. *Sweet!*

"Hello, Uncle!" I smiled broadly and held out my hand. I'd heard Rohit address his elders as *Uncle* and *Aunty* out of respect, even when they weren't directly related to him. I was going to show the Lals I could blend into any culture, like eggs into cake batter.

"No, Dylan—" Mrs. Lal started to say.

"Don't worry, Mrs. L," I whispered. "I know my manners. I won't let you down."

The old man, still wearing pj's in the middle of the day, gaped at me, then scuttled backward. He might have at least gotten dressed given that he was expecting company, but I wasn't fussy. He could have worn a bedsheet and I was still going to be on my very best behavior.

I stepped forward, arm outstretched, feeling like a dork. He took another step back. This man was seriously whacko. Was I going to have to chase him around the flat just to shake his hand? And why wasn't Rohit greeting him, too? A sideways glance revealed my friend's deadpan face and twinkling eyes. I lowered my hand immediately.

"Hello, Rohit. Hello, Priya," a voice boomed out from somewhere behind the old man.

He shuffled away, muttering under his breath about crazy *goras*. Mrs. Lal's lips twitched and Rohit's shoulders heaved with silent laughter.

"What?" I snapped, still annoyed the old man had refused to shake my hand. It was *discrimination*. What did he have against Americans that he couldn't even greet me in a civilized manner? It was the British who had oppressed the Indians for years, not *us*!

"*That* was the servant," Rohit said, his voice shaking with laughter. "I bet no one's ever greeted him this warmly or *respectfully*."

"I tried to tell you, Dylan," said Rohit's mother. "But, no problem. Now even the servant knows you're a very polite boy."

Rohit's bua emerged from the gloom—a slim, distinguished-looking lady wearing a sky-blue saree with orange swirls. She had short gray hair, stylishly cut, and piercing light-gray eyes. Rohit's mother stepped forward and hugged her, then both were talking at once.

"Hello-*ji*," she said, turning her laser-beam vision on me. "You must be Rohit's friend Dylan. Welcome to India." Rohit's aunt gave me a light hug and released me quickly as if I might detonate in her arms. Or contaminate her in some way.

"Hello, er . . . *Aunty*," I said, glancing at Rohit. He gave a small nod.

"Hello, *Beta*," she trilled back, pinching my cheek. "You look like a boy who appreciates food. You've come to the right place!"

I was floored by her insight, though the pinch hurt. "That's absolutely right, Aunty."

"Hello, Rohit!" she said, hugging my friend and almost crushing his glasses. "My, just look at you, all dressed up and acting posh! Don't ever forget your Indian roots, *Beta*, or your poor aunty who has done so much for you and your family."

Mrs. Lal's smile slipped and Rohit's seemed glued onto his face. I had a feeling we were in for a very *interesting* afternoon, and not in a nice way.

Boa (with all the hugging and crushing the name seemed *so* right for her) oozed into the living room, herding us along. A faint odor of ginger and garlic hung in the air. Bright colors bombarded me from every corner. Paintings with Indian maharajahs astride elephants hung on beige walls. Rugs in shades of red and orange lay on the tiled floor. The late afternoon sun slanted through the window, cutting a bright swath on the green cushions artfully strewn on the sofa. Rohit's aunt kept up a nonstop chatter as we made ourselves comfortable.

"What will you have, Dylan?" she asked. "Limca, Fanta, Thums Up, or Mangola?"

I had no idea if these were food or drinks. I looked at Rohit.

"Seven Up, orange Crush, Coke, or a mango drink," he said, translating.

"Or a *lassi*?" Rohit's aunt added.

Ahhh, lassi. Now that was a word I recognized. I'd tried this sweet yogurt drink at Rohit's house and loved it. "I'll have a *lassi*, please. Thank you."

"*Arrey*, what a polite boy," she said. "Smart choice. Very cooling in this heat. Priya, Rohit, what about you?"

"I'll have the same as Dylan, Anjali, thank you," said Mrs. Lal.

"Thums Up for me," said Rohit.

"Oh!" said Boa. "Indian drinks are not good enough for you now, Rohit?"

Rohit's elbows twitched by his side and he blinked rapidly. "What is wrong with choosing a Thums Up?" he snapped. "I prefer it to a *lassi*."

"Rohit," his mother said in a warning tone.

"My, my, what a lot of attitude in one so young," said Boa. "Is this what I paid for, Priya? This rude, disrespectful behavior?"

"Anjali, please," Mrs. Lal said, her gaze flicking toward me. "We have a guest."

They all looked at me. I studied my camera as if I'd found a hitherto undiscovered button that would make me invisible.

"All I want is a cold drink," said Rohit, his voice quivering with anger and growing louder by the second. "If that's too much trouble, please give me a glass of water."

"Be quiet, you silly boy," hissed Boa. "Do you want the neighbors to hear? The walls are paper-thin and most times I can hear exactly what's going on in Mrs. Modi's flat."

For a minute there was silence. Mrs. Lal looked mortified and Rohit's face resembled a thundercloud. Boa tiptoed to the living room wall and pressed her ear against it. If only she were British, she'd perfectly fit the description of Petunia Dursley, Harry Potter's aunt who loved to spy on her neighbors.

I finally understood why Mrs. Lal and Rohit had been apprehensive about meeting *this* particular relative. We hadn't been here five minutes and she'd pissed off both of them. And what did she mean by "Is this what I paid for?" I hated her already.

"Ramu!" Boa hollered. She had tremendous lung power for someone so petite.

The old man appeared with a towel over his shoulder. He eyed me warily as he listened to Rohit's aunt order our preferences, and then shuffled away. Boa started chattering about the upcoming wedding and Mrs. Lal jumped into the conversation with relief and gusto. Rohit and I sat there rolling our eyes at each other. Clothes, wedding, jewelry, the bride, the groom, the menu. They kept interrupting each other and I wondered if either of them was even listening.

My brain had already switched off. I fiddled with my camera again, trying not to look too bored. Rohit caught my eye, winked, and yawned loudly.

"*Tch, tch*, rude again?" Boa said, frowning at Rohit. "Is this what they're teaching in American schools? What a complete waste of my hard-earned money."

"Yes," said Rohit, in a surprising show of defiance. "This is what they're teaching, and much more."

"That's enough, Rohit," Mrs. Lal said, her voice icy. "Anjali, maybe the boys could watch TV for a bit? I'm sure this talk must be . . . um . . . a bit boring for them."

"Yes, please, Aunty," I piped in with my most winning smile. "I love Bollywood movies."

"Of course, of course," Boa said, syrupy all of a sudden. "Go to the dining room through there. I'll send Ramu with your drinks and snacks."

"Thank you," we said in unison and fled.

I felt her eyes follow us out of the room. No wonder Rohit's hackles were up every time she opened her mouth. Even Mrs. Lal's stress made sense now. Boa had a way of twisting words to make her point. And it was *twice* now that she'd mentioned her financial support. She made my dad look positively angelic. I finally got Rohit's reluctance to come back to India to see relatives. The ones I'd met so far were okay, but this one was rotten to the core.

As soon as we'd settled into comfortable chairs, our drinks arrived; mine was a tall glass of frothy yogurt whipped up with salt and sugar, and Rohit's was a boring Thums Up. I took a huge gulp and felt the sweet, tangy drink slide down my parched throat. The colorful food looked delicious: samosas and chutney I recognized, but there was so much more. There were orange and yellow squiggly things, lots of brown and white balls, and cream-colored squares covered in silver. My mouth watered.

"This looks fantastic . . . translate," I asked Rohit, crunching up one of the tidbits.

"What you just ate was a *ghatiya*. Both orange and yellow ones are made of chickpea flour but with different spices," he said. "The white balls are *rasgullas*, the brown balls are *gulab jamuns,* and that silver-covered stuff is *barfi*."

The orange thingamajigs (I couldn't pronounce the names Ro had effortlessly rattled off) were spicy and required a gulp of *lassi* to calm my protesting taste buds. The fat yellow worm-looking things with serrated edges were spiced with cumin and were delish, too. I couldn't believe something that sounded like *barf* could taste good, but this sure did! My absolute favorites were what Ro told me later were called *jalebis*: orange sweets coiled like mini-snakes that oozed sugar syrup as soon as you bit into them.

We piled our plates high and settled back. Rohit turned on the TV and the screen seemed to explode with sound and picture. Bandits were chasing a train speeding through a deserted landscape. A policeman and two civilians were shooting at them with rifles and missing most of the time. Thumping music matched the action. I watched and munched.

"Pass the chutney, please," I asked Rohit.

He passed me the bowl and I drowned my samosa in it. "Want some?" I said.

"Nah," he said, not looking away from the screen. "Chutney of any sort doesn't agree with me."

"More for me," I said, taking a huge bite of my potato-pea samosa. I thought I'd died and gone to food heaven.

Just as one of the bandits caught up with the train, Rohit changed the channel.

"Why'd you do that?" I said. "Go back."

"This is an *ancient* movie . . . *Sholay*," he said. "Let's see if we can find an English channel. It'll have better programs."

"I want to watch this one, Ro," I said. "C'mon, be a sport."

"Really?" asked Rohit. "You won't understand a word and there are no subtitles."

"I don't care," I said, waving a half-eaten *jalebi* at him. "Now go back to *Sholly* or whatever you called it, before we miss the end of that fight."

Rohit flipped back to the movie with a deep sigh. I snuck a glance at him after a few minutes. A *jalebi* was inches away from his open mouth, syrup puddling on his plate while he goggled at the screen. I wanted to take a picture and wave it in his face—evidence that he still enjoyed these *ancient* movies in spite of his vehement protests—but I let it go.

Rohit translated the dialogue during the slow parts. But the actions were so exaggerated, I really didn't need much help. As always there were lots of songs, and multiple set and clothing changes within a four-minute window—a physical impossibility unless they'd learned to teleport.

And there was the running. A lot of running—around trees, in meadows, on the beach, and down a hill. It dawned on me that Bollywood actors had to be in really good shape. Feeling a little guilty, I put aside my plate and did a few push-ups, crunches, and jumping jacks. Rohit watched with the smug smile of a person who wouldn't know how to *spell* diet. His high metabolism meant he could eat anything without getting fat, the lucky idiot.

Unfortunately, in just a few minutes I was panting like a Saint Bernard crossing the Sahara desert.

Note to Self: Looking like you're in shape and being in shape are completely different. The two better be the same before you head back to New York.

But the *jalebis* beckoned. I abandoned my exercise and went back to eating.

"Why is the girl dancing on broken glass with bare feet while singing?" I said. "Is she completely nuts?"

"Welcome to Bollywood," Rohit said. "Her love for her man is so deep, she will dance for him in spite of the broken glass because if she stops the bandit will shoot him."

"I see," I said. But really, I didn't see at all. It seemed kind of pointless to me and cruel on the bandit's part. I couldn't wait for the song to end. It seemed just the right time for a bathroom break. Rohit was zoned out so I decided to find it on my own.

I wandered back toward the living room and ended up eavesdropping on a conversation between Mrs. Lal and Boa. I didn't *mean* to but, once I got the gist of it, I had to stay and hear the rest. I listened, more horrified and chilled with each passing second.

FOUR

I STOOD QUIETLY JUST OUTSIDE THE LIVING ROOM
where Mrs. Lal and Boa were still talking, hoping Ramu
wouldn't discover me and give me away.

"The Indian education system is the *best*," Boa said. "He's
learning all this *altu-faltu* stuff from the American school and
picking up attitude he can do without. I cannot continue to
pay for this nonsense, Priya."

"But he loves it there and he's made friends with Dylan,"
Mrs. Lal said. "It was tough for him to leave three years ago
and settle down. How can you ask me to uproot him again?"

"*Tch, tch,* boys are tough," said Boa. "He will stay with me
and attend the best school in Mumbai. I'll send him back to
attend university in the States, which, of course, I will continue to finance."

Pregnant pause here, after which she added softly, "Besides,
Priya, I'm all alone here. I have money but no family. Can you
understand why I am asking this?"

For a moment I knew *exactly* where she was coming from.
Money could never take away loneliness, and in a way, her

situation was similar to mine. I had everything money could buy but only one true friend. But what she was suggesting would make a lot of people unhappy, especially me.

Mrs. Lal spoke up then. "I do understand, Anjali, but that does not mean you have the right to break up my family. You're being very selfish."

I heard a sharp intake of breath. "I understand that university fees can run into tens of thousands of dollars," said Boa. "It's in your best interest to keep me happy."

Just from the tone, I could imagine the poisonous snake reclining on the sofa, her forked tongue flicking in and out as she blackmailed Mrs. Lal. I was angry on her behalf but I felt worse for Rohit. He had no idea what was being plotted.

"I'll talk to Arun about it," said Boa. "My brother won't refuse me."

"No, *I'll* talk to my husband about it," Mrs. Lal said coldly. "It's a family decision but I will say this, Anjali. I hate you pressuring us like this."

My respect for Mrs. Lal shot up. She was one tough lady.

"You talk, I talk—it doesn't matter," said Boa. "As long as the outcome is what *I* want, I really don't care what you think."

All this because Rohit chose a Thums Up over a *lassi*? What would have happened if he'd asked for chocolate cake instead of *jalebis*?

No way was Mrs. Lal leaving her son behind. But what if she did? From the conversation, it sounded like Boa was used to getting her way. Always. If that happened, Mrs. Lal would suffer but I'd be a total goner! Bathroom forgotten, I raced back to tell Rohit.

"You sure you heard right?" said Rohit, his face pale.

"Loud and clear, bro," I said. "But Boa can't be serious, can she?"

For a moment we stared at the TV screen. Rohit blinked rapidly and I could almost see the wheels turning in his head. After a few moments he sank back into the chair. "Nah, I don't think Ma will do this. I'm her one and only. I don't think she can survive without me."

"What's this financial help she keeps throwing in your faces?" I asked. From all the conversations I'd overheard, I knew money was important to adults—those who had it wielded power, and those who didn't got bullied.

"Bua is filthy rich," said Rohit bitterly. "We're not. She financed our move to the States and she never lets us forget it. She thinks it gives her the right to run our lives."

"So she could easily force your parents to leave you behind?" I said, sick to my stomach and in desperate need of the bathroom.

Rohit was quiet for a moment. "Papa, yes. Ma, no. Ma hates her ever since she found out Bua had tried to stop Papa from marrying her because she believed Ma was trying to steal her baby brother away from her."

The band around my chest loosened and I could breathe again. "So nothing to worry about, dude?"

Rohit slurped his Thums Up. "Not a thing."

Turned out he was dead wrong.

Rohit's mom and aunt entered the room. Boa talked so fast the words melded together, sounding like an Indian version of Parseltongue. Mrs. Lal nodded occasionally but didn't say much.

"Time to go, boys," said Mrs. Lal. She looked tired and I felt sorry for her. Boa had wrung her dry with all the heartless things she'd said, and the blackmail she was planning. I hoped Mrs. Lal would stay strong. Our fellowship rested in her tiny hands.

"Thank you, Aunty," I said politely. "The snacks were delicious."

"You are most welcome, Dylan," she replied, her tone syrupy. "Come back anytime."

"Thanks, Bua," Rohit said. "The Thums Up was great."

His aunt nodded at him coolly, and then shot a knowing look at Mrs. Lal. If I hadn't overheard the conversation, her glance might have gone unnoticed. Now that I knew she was trying to break up our friendship and my friend's family, I couldn't stand to be near her for one more second. She truly was a snake.

The sidewalks were even more packed this time of the evening. People spilled onto the main road and our cabbie drove with his head perpetually stuck out the window, yelling at pedestrians to get out of the way. Honking had no effect at all.

Kerosene lamps smoked, a temple bell at a roadside shrine tinkled, and the air was thick with smells—some good, some gross. Rohit swore softly under his breath as the cab inched forward. After being in the air-conditioned flat, the heat was borderline torture. It was like being in a malfunctioning steam room with the temperature stuck on *cook*. My face was burning with the heat and probably beet red.

"Almost there," said Rohit's mother, staring at me with concern. "If we walk, we'll reach the flat faster. Then you can have a cool shower, okay, Dylan?"

"Uh-huh," I said, too hot even to speak.

We piled out of the cab and were sucked into the fast-moving stream of people on the sidewalk. I felt a stab of fear. If I got lost now, I'd never find my way back to the flat. I moved closer to Rohit, my fingers surreptitiously brushing the hem of his T-shirt, ready to grab him if need be. New York was crowded, too, but Mumbai took crowded to a whole new level. I was being smothered in hot and sweaty bodies.

"We shouldn't visit anyone at peak traffic times, Ma," said Rohit as we struggled against hordes of people heading home. "This place is worse than I remembered it."

I was too busy trying not to get swept away to tell Rohit to shut up. Now I knew what a salmon went through every year and I developed the greatest respect for them. The next time I ordered one, I'd salute the salmon before digging in.

"Don't *you* start telling me what to do!" said Mrs. Lal,

looking thoroughly annoyed. "I've already had an earful from your bua!"

"Then why didn't we wait till Papa got here before visiting her?" said Rohit. "We both can't stand her so why go through this torture?"

He had a point. They both did. But Rohit was my friend and I was always going to take his side, no matter what. I knew he hadn't wanted to come here on vacation or for the wedding. He'd asked (begged, actually) to spend the three weeks his parents were away in India with me; I'd counterbegged him, saying that I needed to get away from home desperately. He'd relented and asked his mom to invite me to Mumbai.

He'd put my needs before his and hadn't asked too many questions, which was another thing I appreciated about Rohit. He never pushed, letting me share my reasons at my own pace. I felt guilty that I still hadn't figured out how or when to tell him about my own miserable situation. But right now he had enough to deal with, especially with Boa insisting he stay back in Mumbai to finish school. I just wished he wouldn't speak his mind quite so freely because he was playing right into Boa's coils. Sam would have to prevail to save Frodo from a fate worse than death.

"I am your mother and you will speak to me with respect."

"I can't wait to get back to New York, and then I won't have to speak to you at all," said Rohit.

"That's what you think," she snapped.

We were straying into dangerous territory here and the very air seemed to crackle with electricity.

"What exactly is that supposed to mean?" said Rohit. He stopped in the middle of the road and glared at his mother. I knew he was waiting for her to disclose the conversation she'd just had with Boa.

People bumped into us and cursed as they hurried away. If we'd been cows, they would have given us a wide berth, even thrown in a *namaste*. But we were mere mortals obstructing foot traffic and we got a few choice expletives instead.

Mrs. Lal glared back at Rohit silently. I swear I could see steam shooting out of her ears. Diversionary tactics were needed *immediately*. I took a deep breath and stepped into the nearest pile of poop.

"Is cow dung sacred, too?" I asked, trying not to grimace. "I mean can you get beaten up for disturbing the sacred Mother's crap?"

That got their attention in a hurry. Mother and son stared at me as if I'd gone crazy.

"What?" asked Rohit.

"Because I just stepped in some," I said, raising my foot an inch off the sidewalk. The sole and side of my shoe were covered in brown goo and, man, did it stink. Rohit owed me, big-time.

"Oh, Dylan, what is it with you and cows?" said Mrs. Lal, shaking her head ruefully.

"Accident," I said, shrugging.

"Scrape your shoe against the curb and we'll wash it when we get home."

Rohit's mouth curved into a grin as he followed his mother. "You stink, dude. That's twice in one day."

It made dirtying my expensive Nikes worthwhile.

Rohit's mom was smiling, too. "Dylan, there is nothing sacred about cow dung, though it is very useful in villages as biodegradable fuel. But here's something interesting. The Parsees induct a person into their religion by having them drink the pee of a sacred cow."

"You're pulling my leg, Mrs. L, aren't you?" People drinking cow pee? *Beyond gross*. But this tactic had successfully averted a meltdown between the two and I was all for keeping it going for as long as I could.

"I'm serious, Dylan. The Parsees conduct the *Navjote* ceremony when a child comes of age at about seven or eight. And part of the ceremony is to drink cow's pee. Except, this is a sacred cow kept in an enclosure and fed on the best grass. So there are supposed to be no, umm . . . impurities in her pee."

"Wow!" I hurried along, trying to make sure the crap didn't dirty my other shoe. "What a great topic for a school project." I made a mental note to Google it when I had the time.

Just as we started up the steps to the flat, something the size of a black kitten zipped past my leg. I jumped a foot in the air. Rohit's mother squeaked and sprinted up to the first floor. The black shadow streaked to the doorway and disappeared into the darkening street.

My heart flopped like a dying fish in my chest. "What was that?" I said.

"A rat," said Mrs. Lal with a grimace. "I had forgotten how big they were!"

"It must have been a cat, Mrs. L. It was huge!"

Mrs. Lal shook her head. "The cats are even bigger. They have to be if they want to survive the rats."

"The gutters are open in this old part of Mumbai," said Rohit. "Rats get plenty of food, so they're very healthy."

We'd reached the second-floor landing and Mrs. Lal dug around inside her purse for the key. Rohit leaned against the wall and looked at me as I peered into the gloom on the dimly lit staircase. "Do you know they can even climb up drainpipes and get into flats?"

Laughter echoed in my ears as we piled into the humid flat. I knew I'd be dreaming about monster rats that night. I loved Ro's dry sense of humor, but there were times when I could have strangled him for TMI. This time *definitely* qualified.

FIVE

MRS. LAL OFFERED TO CLEAN MY SHOE AND I GRATE-
fully accepted. Having inhaled the stench all the way
home, I couldn't handle it for another second. Once I'd depos-
ited it in the bathroom after a quick shower, I lay on the tiled
floor of the living room and stared up at the ceiling fan. Even
though it was set to full speed, it wasn't making any difference. I would have put up with Boa for her air-conditioned
flat but decided to suck it up and, more importantly, shut up.
Two of us whining was going to be majorly boring.

A damp washcloth landed on my cheek, splattering cold
water down my neck. I covered my face with it, grateful for
the slight relief. Rohit lay down on the floor beside me with a
cloth on his face, too. "Better?"

"Much," I said.

Then we were silent, two weary souls contemplating the
mysteries of the universe. Actually I was wondering what was
for dinner and I knew what was on Rohit's mind.

"You still thinking of Boa and having to stay back?" I asked.

"Because that's not going to happen. I don't see your mom giving in."

"I'll go nuts if I have to stay here. I *hate* this place."

"Why?" I folded the washcloth into a strip and laid it across my forehead.

"Where do I even begin," said Rohit with a deep sigh.

"Sam's got no pressing engagements at the moment, Frodo. Go for it."

Rohit snorted. Any fantasy movie or book reference, but especially *Lord of the Rings*, was guaranteed to get a reaction out of him. Ditto for me. We really were nerds of a feather.

"Go on," I said. "I'd like to understand how you can hate a place you lived most of your life. I *love* this place, heat, cow crap, and all. Except Boa, of course. You just gotta look at the good stuff and ignore the bad."

"Come on," said Rohit. He raised himself, balancing on one elbow. The washcloth slid off his face. Without his glasses his eyes looked kind of squinty and weird. "We don't even have an air conditioner! It must be quite the adventure experiencing how the other half lives, but why pretend you like it? I wish you'd just tell the truth so we can get back to New York early. In fact, I think you should tell Ma *tonight*. Tell her you can't handle the heat and the crowds. Then Boa won't have time to pressure Ma or Papa. We all win."

Rohit's face was red and blotchy. I knew he was ashamed of his flat compared with my brownstone, and torturing himself thinking of all the things I must *miss*. I thought of Mrs. Lal and how important it was for her to be at the wedding. How could I ruin it by telling her to cut the trip short? I had a strong feeling she might even agree to go back early if she thought I was miserable. She was *that* sweet.

The truth was, I didn't want to go home any time soon. I'd do anything to postpone the misery of what awaited me. But staying meant my best bud was going to have a miserable summer with the threat of being left behind hanging over him like the proverbial sword-neck scenario. How was I going to keep them both happy and get what I wanted, too?

"I love your flat, most of your family, and everything I've seen so far. You can choose to believe me or not," I said finally, deciding to stick with the truth. "I'm not ready to go back yet."

"Why?" said Rohit. He sat up and looked me in the eye. "Something's up and you're not telling me."

He'd opened the door. I only had to walk through it. But I hesitated. I still wasn't ready to talk about it. "If I go back early, Mom's going to send me to a camp where they make you wake up at an unholy hour to take a swim. Or Dad will make me go to the office with him or join a soccer camp. Do you hate me so much that you'd condemn me to that torture?"

"Yes!" he said, half smiling, half annoyed. "Better you than me. Seriously, Dylan, what're you hiding? You know I know something's up so you might as well spill it."

"Me hide something from you?" I said in mock horror. "Never! I think you're pushing me just so you can win your bet. Not a chance, Ro. I'm staying the entire three weeks."

Rohit crossed his arms over his chest and continued to stare at me. His gaze was as impossible to escape as the all-seeing eye of Sauron. I knew I'd have to give him something, if not the whole truth.

"There's this photography competition I want to enter," I said, choosing my words carefully. "It's run by *National Geographic Kids*. Had a bet with Dad that I could win *something*."

Rohit was still giving me the evil eye. I continued.

"The first prize is a fantastic family vacation; I'm trying to win it to show him I'm a good photographer." *And save my parents' marriage*. But I didn't say that out loud.

"And you can't take a winning photograph in the States? Who do you think I am—Neville Longbottom?"

I was annoyed and proud at the same time. I hadn't picked an idiot for a friend but did he have to see through my story so easily? I'd have to try harder.

"Look around you, Ro. This place has more exotic stuff in one square mile than half of New York. Why settle for the ordinary when I have access to all this?" I waved my arms energetically to encompass the flat, Mumbai, and India.

"Tell me more about this bet with your dad," said Rohit.

"He thinks I'm wasting my time with photography and it's not a hobby that helps a person get into shape. I'm going to prove him wrong on both counts. Now, are you going to help me or quiz me to death?"

"And if you don't win?" said Rohit, staring at me from the top of his glasses, which were now at the tip of his nose. Ro was as relentless as Voldemort and his constant attempts to kill Harry.

"I'll have to join a soccer league and try out for the team in the fall."

"Dude, you *hate* team sports," said Rohit, twitching in sympathy. "That's torture."

"I rest my case," I said. "*Now* do you get why we have to stay, why I have to try and win, and get in shape so that Dad notices and gets off my case?"

Rohit lay back down on the tile floor and adjusted the cloth over his face. "Hmmm," he said. "Hmmmmmm."

"You gonna say something or just hum away uselessly?"

"All right," he said. "I'll help you if you'll help me."

"Deal," I said, glad he'd bought it. It *was* the partial truth so I didn't feel too bad withholding the really important part.

"You know what else you could do," said Rohit.

"Listening."

"You could put the really good ones up for sale on iStock— the photography website. Make a bit of extra cash on the side. Your dad will be impressed with your entrepreneurial flair and you'll be able to afford more equipment on your own."

"Bro, did I ever tell you, you're brilliant!"

"Wouldn't mind hearing it again," said Rohit.

"Forget it."

Delicious smells wafted out of the kitchen as we lay side by side on the floor. Over the clink of pots and pans, I heard Mrs. Lal hum a tune. The excited shrieks of kids playing in the street and sounds of traffic leaked into the flat. Being surrounded by activity and life kept the loneliness at bay but thoughts about home crept in anyway.

One dinner a couple of months before summer break. I was in my beautiful, quiet-as-a-morgue kitchen. Eating alone. Mom was at one of her many social commitments and Dad was still at work. Maria, our maid slash housekeeper, had made pork chops with mashed potatoes, grilled veggies, and mushroom gravy. There was a chocolate soufflé in the oven for dessert. She asked me if I wanted anything else and I was desperate to tell her I needed company. But she was so eager to Skype with her family back in the Philippines that she was already talking about it. As soon as I shook my head she took off, her footsteps echoing through the empty house, all the way to the servants' quarters. I ate dinner in silence, with Death for company. (I was reading The Book Thief *by Markus Zusak.) After I finished eating I put my plate in the dishwasher, turned off the lights, and went to my room, Death clutched in my hand.*

If I cut my vacation short, that was what I was going back to. I closed my eyes, fighting back the urge to cry. I couldn't go back. Not yet.

"Dylan?"

"Yes, Mrs. L?"

"Would you like to eat Bombay ducks tonight? I bought them from the fisherwoman this morning. They're fresh and very tasty."

"Duck sounds swag, Mrs. L. Yes, please!"

"Good. You boys watch TV, or play a game. Dinner will be ready in an hour. Rohit, take this lemonade for you and Dylan."

"I'll get it," I said, sitting up.

Rohit flicked up a thumb, making no attempt to move.

"Anything else I can help with, Mrs. L?" I asked as I entered the kitchen. It was the size of our guest bathroom back home and every surface was covered with pots, cutting boards, and an array of spice jars. There was no sign of the duck and I assumed it was in the oven. "I'm quite good in the kitchen."

Mrs. Lal laughed. "No, thank you, Dylan. But surely you must have a cook at home given that Rosemary is so busy with her work."

So busy that she has no time for me. "We do, Mrs. L, but I make a mean shrimp fried rice."

Rohit's mother stared at me. "Mean?"

"A very good one," I explained.

"You boys and your funny words," she said, smiling. "One of these days I'm going to speak using my own slang. Then you'll realize just how confusing it is. But seriously, you know how to cook?"

I nodded. "I love to eat, so I like to experiment with different cuisines."

"Admirable," said Mrs. Lal. "I think all boys should learn how to cook. A handy skill at any time, but especially in university. I'm sure your mother must be very impressed with you."

Impressed? Another miserable evening at home, now indelibly etched in my mind, came back to me.

I'd just told Dad I wanted to take professional photography classes with Ari Valokuva and be like him someday.

At first Dad had laughed but when I didn't join in, he stopped. "Son, team sports, like soccer, teach life skills. Photography teaches you nothing. It's a girl's hobby."

"I don't think so," I said and watched his jaw clench, the all-too-familiar vein in his temple throb.

"Do you know how I got where I am today?" he said as calmly as he could manage.

"You've mentioned it," I said. "A few hundred times already." I knew talking back could set him off in a minute, but his comment about photography being for girls hurt.

"There's no need to be rude," Dad snapped. "Rosemary, you should teach your son some manners."

"He's your son, too," Mom said. "Why don't you stick around some more and lead by example."

For a moment they glared at each other, ready to rip out each other's throats. Mom recovered first and took a deep breath.

"Dylan, are you serious about this?"

"Yes. I've told you before, I hate team sports but especially soccer."

"How can you know, when you've never tried?" Dad asked.

"I did, Dad. A while ago. It's just not my thing." There was no way I was opening that can of worms. The way the class laughed at my clumsy attempts to kick the ball into the net. The more they heckled, the wider I kicked.

"I'll get you the best soccer coach money can buy," he said. "You'll see, once you become good, it's addictive. You'll want to play soccer every spare minute you get. You'll also be in great shape. Double ROI, I say."

"That's how I feel about photography. That's why all I've asked for, for my birthday, has been camera equipment."

"I don't see you winning anything."

"That's all life's about for you," said Mom. "Winning, no matter what the cost. And you want our son to be like that?"

"What's wrong with winning?" he asked. "I don't see you complaining about the luxurious lifestyle you're enjoying with my money."

They were circling again, snarling and ready to pounce. It was exhausting to watch them. And depressing.

"I'd complain if you were around long enough to listen to me," Mom almost yelled.

Dad was red-faced by now, clenching and unclenching his fists. He strode off, muttering to himself about how he wanted only the best for his family but they were too selfish and blind to see it. Thankless! Ungrateful!

Mom sipped her wine, staring into space.

"Mom, is everything okay between you and Dad? You're both fighting a lot."

Mom chugged the wine in one go, put down the glass, and looked at me. "No matter what happens between me and your father, remember that we love you."

I'd watched enough movies to know exactly what this meant. Divorce.

"Do you agree with Dad, about the photography?" I asked, watching her.

"You know I'll support you no matter what, Dylan. But your dad needs a win."

"I'll win," I said. "I'll show him."

"My Rohit couldn't boil an egg," said Mrs. Lal, stirring the pot of lentils on the stove, unaware that I wasn't paying attention. She added a handful of chopped cilantro to it. The earthy fragrance of the herb mingled with the lentils, filling the kitchen with an aroma that made my taste buds tingle. "Dylan, are you okay? You look a little pale."

"Yep!" I said, recovering quickly. "And I'm sure Rohit could boil an egg if he had to but with a mom like you . . . he doesn't need to. Lucky guy!"

Mrs. Lal stopped what she was doing and looked at me. Not distractedly, the way Mom did while typing away on her iPad, or Dad, who nodded while still glancing at the *Wall Street Journal*. Mrs. Lal looked at me with complete focus. It made me feel like I was the most important person in the world. She touched my shoulder gently. "You're lucky, too, Dylan, and I'm sure your parents feel the same way even if they don't say it out loud."

I gave her a spontaneous hug. She smiled and returned it. Neither of my parents had said that they were proud of me in a long time, if ever. Mom, in her usual anti-PDA style, rarely hugged. Even though I knew she loved me, a peck on the cheek was the most I could expect from her. If I was a new kind of building material, Dad would have showered me with love and affection. But I was his nonathletic son who took up girly hobbies instead of manly ones like soccer.

"Thanks, Mrs. L."

"Here, take the lemonade. Dinner will be ready soon."

I walked out of the kitchen, sipping the tangy, sweet drink and feeling better.

While Rohit aimlessly flicked through TV channels, I decided to catch up on my email. The Lals had bought a temporary plan for Internet and cell coverage for our short stay, though I seemed to be getting the most use out of it.

There was an email from Mom telling me she missed me and asking how I'd survived the first week in Mumbai. Nothing from Dad. I typed a short response saying I was fine, that I missed her, too, and clicked send.

There was one from *National Geographic*. I wiped my sweaty palms on my shorts and clicked on it. *"Sweet!"* This was just the opportunity I wanted—needed—to prove to my parents I wasn't wasting my time.

Rohit sat up immediately. "What?"

"*National Geographic Kids* just announced this year's photo contest theme and it's open for submissions. First prize is that cool family vacation I mentioned."

"What's the theme?"

I smiled. "Friendship."

Rohit smiled back. "Think you really have a shot at winning?"

"I'm in a crazy-exciting city with my best friend. How could I not?"

We bumped fists as my mind catalogued all the photographs I'd taken so far. I knew I'd have to take more now that I had direction, but the sweetest picture of them all would be the look on my parents' faces when I told them I'd won the contest. I knew I could, if I tried.

"I'll help you win!" said Rohit.

"And *I'll* help get Boa off your back," I said. "Any ideas so far?"

Rohit's smile sagged. "Uh-uh. You go first."

"Okay, here's a thought," I said, taking a long swig of my lemonade. "Your aunt's main argument is that American schools have ruined your attitude and behavior and she's wasting her money. She thinks keeping you here to finish school will solve that problem. What if you're so well behaved that the basis of her argument is shattered? Then if she insists, she's just going to sound petty and your dad will see it, too."

"Nice try, but no," said Rohit. "Here's my plan. Ma's got a really short fuse. She can't tolerate bad behavior for very long and hates being embarrassed in front of relatives and friends. If I make her really mad at me she might pack up and take the first flight back to New York. She'll give me hell for it but at least we'll be back home."

"Trust me!" I said. "*My* way, your mom gets to attend the wedding, and she realizes your respectful roots still stretch all the way from New York to Mumbai. *And* I get to stay here and find my winning picture. Everyone's cool!"

Rohit stared at me for a few minutes while I prayed he'd agree. If we did it his way, we'd all have a horrible time and I'd have to go home sooner. I couldn't face that.

"Okay," he said, finally. "We do it your way. But it better work."

"It will," I said with more confidence that I actually felt. "I promise."

"Dinner's ready," Rohit's mother called out. "Can you boys help me carry all the food to the dining table?"

I shut my laptop and hurried to the kitchen. *Bombay ducks, here I come.* Within minutes we were all sitting down. I scanned the table for a humongous duck or even a couple of scrawny ones. There were brown lentils, fluffy white rice with melted butter, and cauliflower with peas. On a white plate lay a dozen small eel-like fish, as long as my palm, with a golden coating. *Interesting little side dish.* But no duck.

"Er, Mrs. Lal, where's the duck?" I asked.

"Right there," she said, pointing to the eel-like thingies.

"Ma, he's thinking of a regular duck," said Rohit, grinning. "Right?"

"I—um—this is a *duck*?" I said, trying to hide my confusion. "No offense but it looks more like a snake on a diet."

Rohit patted me on the back. "Nothing in life is what it seems, my friend."

I stared at the duck, feeling a bit cheated.

"Never judge a duck by its size," said Mrs. Lal, smiling. "Try it. You'll love it."

I almost rolled my eyes but caught myself at the last minute. I didn't want to hurt her feelings. I took a couple of close-ups first (Mom would love to know what a *duck* in India looked like), then slid one onto my plate and dug my fork into the crisp brown skin. It fell off easily to reveal tender white flesh and a translucent spine. I scooped up a bit with my fork and sniffed it. It *smelled* all right. I popped it into my mouth and my taste buds did the tango. This weird skinny "duck" had a delicate, sweet flavor with a hint of spice and lemon. It was soft and crunchy all at once.

"Like it?" asked Rohit, helping himself to one.

"*Love* it! Where have you been hiding these little beauties, Mrs. L?" I wolfed them down. One, two, four, six. I couldn't stop. They were that good.

"Slow down, Dylan," said Mrs. Lal, frowning. "It's a new food and you don't know how your stomach is going to react to it. Have some lentils and rice, too."

"My stomach," I said, taking another bite, "will be just fine." And I devoured three more in quick succession. Huge mistake.

That night my stomach had a lot to say about having an alien food shoved into it. So it shoved the food right back . . . out. I spent most of the night in the bathroom fighting an explosive duck situation. Ron belching slugs in *The Chamber of Secrets* looked like a picnic compared to what happened to me. Let's just say I'll be having nightmares about Bombay ducks for a long time.

Note to Self: Always listen to Mrs. L!

SIX

PLANS FOR NISHA'S WEDDING WERE IN FULL SWING over the next few days. Rohit didn't seem overly excited about his cousin getting married but his family more than compensated for his lack of enthusiasm. There were get-togethers every single day as family poured in from all over India, the UK, Europe, and Australia to celebrate. It was exhausting yet fascinating to watch his relatives try to impress one another with detailed accounts of the wealth and success they'd achieved abroad. Many spoke with the accents of their adopted homes; some sounded real, some as fake as a thirty-dollar bill. The clothes they wore were eye-popping and headache-inducing, colorful with a good amount of gold and silver embroidery. I couldn't stop clicking pictures and faithfully downloaded them onto my laptop every night, showing a few of the best ones to Mrs. Lal and Rohit. One of them had to be a gem that would win me the competition and my dad's respect. The rest were going on iStock for some extra cash thanks to Rohit's brilliant suggestion.

"Rohit, I'm out of tomatoes for my curry," Mrs. Lal called out from the kitchen on a day when you could have cooked an omelet on the sidewalk. "Can you go to the bazaar and get me a few, please?"

Rohit frowned. I knew exactly what was going to pop out of his mouth. I caught his eye and shook my head. *Stick to the plan,* I mouthed.

"Sure, Ma," said Rohit, trying to sound enthusiastic. "How many do you need? Is there anything else I can pick up while I'm out?"

Mrs. Lal stood in the kitchen doorway, clutching a paring knife while she gaped at her son. I could understand her shock. This was a one-eighty from the whiny Rohit of a few days ago. Mother and son were getting along great and I was getting all the pictures I needed as Ro went out of his way to help me explore the area around the flat. Things were working out well and life was good.

"Thank you, *Beta,*" Mrs. Lal sniffed, still standing in the doorway, staring at Rohit. "A few tomatoes are all I need."

"Ma, are you crying?"

"Onions!" she said, shaking her head. "Just cutting onions."

Neither of us pointed out that she was holding a potato.

• • • • • •

Nisha's engagement ceremony was tonight. Every single relative—except Mr. Lal—would be there. I got ready by clearing my memory card and experimenting with a few different lenses that would give me soft, fish-eye, or wide-angle effects on the pictures.

Mrs. Lal fluttered around, trying on one saree after another while bombarding us with admonishments on how to behave at the reception.

"Remember to greet everyone properly," she said, glancing at Rohit. "Mr. and Dr. Ramachandran are old-fashioned. Make sure you do a *namaste* when I introduce you. Don't even try to shake hands with them—they'll be very offended."

"Okay, Ma."

"Aunty Lalita likes to smooch everyone on the lips by way of greeting. She thinks it's sophisticated. Stay well out of range when I introduce you and I'll grab her as soon as she starts leaning in."

"Okay, Ma," said Rohit, holding his head in his hands.

"I wish your father were here," she said softly, worry cutting deep grooves in her normally unlined forehead. "I don't want to do this alone. They'll all be watching us. Judging us." She shuffled into the bedroom.

"They're jealous, Ma," said Rohit. "So why should we care what they think of us?" He was sprawled on the sofa, sipping lemonade, barely paying attention to a Bollywood movie playing on TV. I sat at the dining table, cleaning my camera. I had to clean the lenses every day to make sure I wouldn't ruin a good picture with an errant speck of dust.

Mrs. Lal strode out of the bedroom, her heels clacking on the tiled floor. "This is your dad's family and he cares a lot about their opinions. He's counting on us to make a good impression. Many of his relatives had told him not to leave for the States but he didn't listen. We have to prove that we haven't changed."

"But, Mrs. L, you *have* changed," I said. "Why pretend otherwise?"

She sighed deeply. "It's difficult to explain, Dylan. People who immigrate and come back to visit are *always* judged by how deep their cultural roots go. It's progressive if someone living here adopts the Western culture, but when you actually live in the West you're expected to be more 'Indian' or you're labeled a snob. It's . . . complicated."

"It's not complicated, Ma, it's *nuts*," said Rohit. "But as long as we go back after these three weeks of madness, I'll do whatever you say."

Mrs. Lal gave him a sharp look, which came to rest on me. I wondered if she'd guessed we knew about the conversation between her and Boa but luckily she didn't comment on it further.

"I'm with Rohit on this one, Mrs. L," I said. "This is very weird."

Mrs. Lal poured herself a glass of lemonade from the jug on the table. "Crazy or not, that's the way it is! Rohit, Dylan, tonight is an important event. Do *not* do anything to embarrass me or your father. Bua is mad at us anyway so take special care not to antagonize her any more. In fact, stay as far away from her as possible."

Rohit listened to her carefully and then did exactly the opposite, ruining all our plans.

· · · · · · ·

Soft music wafted through the massive chandelier-adorned lobby of the Oberoi Towers. Gold fixtures glittered in the muted light and lilies perfumed the air. We took a gleaming steel elevator to the basement level where a pulse-pounding, teeth-jarring Bollywood song greeted us long before we reached the engagement party in the Frangipani Banquet Hall.

"Looks like the party's already started," said Rohit, wincing.

"Wow, that's loud," I said. "Guess once people's eardrums are shot, they really can't figure out if the music is good or bad."

As soon as we walked through the doors, I stopped to gape. At the back of the giant hall were two sweet speakers turned up to full volume. In the middle was a single raised platform decorated with red roses. Nisha, in a shimmery gold saree, stood at the center of the platform with Sanjay, smiling at everyone. The room swirled with light and color from people's clothes, silver food platters, and massive chandeliers vibrating with the pounding bass of the music.

"I should have brought my sunglasses," I yelled in Rohit's ear, blinking hard. Almost all the women were laden with jewelry from head to toe. I wondered how they managed to stay upright, never mind move.

"We have to meet a lot of people and pay our respects," said Mrs. Lal, scanning the room. "Come along!"

She looked regal in a deep-maroon silk saree with a gold border, but her eyes were clouded with worry. I felt her pain. No one should have to stress out this much about seeing family and friends. For a moment I could almost appreciate my own relatives. No matter how weird they were, Mom and Dad never looked so worried at family gatherings. Even Rohit, with his twitching arms and glasses perpetually perched at the end of his nose, looked more uncomfortable than usual.

"Ma, do we have to go with you?" said Rohit. "Why don't we wander around on our own so we don't end up shaking hands with the Ramachandrans, or smooching Aunty Lalita?"

"Please, Mrs. L?" I piped in, raising my camera. "I'd like to get some candid shots."

"Okay, but stay in the hall and please do *not*—"

"Embarrass you in any way," Rohit cut in. "Got it. You go have fun."

She nodded and walked away toward a bunch of ladies in psychedelic outfits.

"Will we ever find her again?" I asked Rohit. Crowds were gathering and getting denser by the second.

"Don't worry. Ma will find us when it's time to go. Hungry?"

"Always," I said. My nose had picked up the most delicious fragrances from the far corner of the room. We galloped toward the buffet in as dignified a manner as we could manage.

"Describe," I said to Rohit, my mouth filling with saliva at the array of food.

In under a minute he named them all. We grabbed a plate each and piled them high. I had yet to meet a sweet or snack in India that wasn't scrumptious. Indians believed in coloring their world vividly, even when it came to food. Everything on the table had a vibrant hue and oozed flavor and fragrance.

I added dollops of green and red chutneys on my plate and was just about to add some to Rohit's plate when he held it away.

"Not for me, thanks," he said. "Think I have an allergy to that stuff. Always makes me barf."

"Sorry, forgot!" I said, adding an extra dollop on my samosa.

"Ahhh, Rohit Lal and his friend from *Noo Yark*," said a simpering voice behind us.

We turned around slowly. A monster in a purple saree and black lipstick stood there. I almost hurled my plate, Frisbee-style, to stop her from coming any closer.

"Ackk," I said softly.

"Relax," said Rohit. "It's only Aunty Rita."

"Definitely not," I whispered. "Your aunty has been devoured by Jabba the Hutt's sister. We're next."

"*Haylooo*, my dears," she said, reaching out with purple talons. She pinched my cheeks hard, bringing tears to my eyes.

I desperately wanted to pinch her back and only respect for Mrs. Lal (and her instructions) kept my fingers in check.

"How are you enjoying India, dear?" she said, blasting me with garlic breath. I almost passed out.

"Great, Mrs. . . . . er," I said, inching backward.

"Call me Aunty. I see you like our humble food," she said, stepping closer. I backed up. She reached out again with those deadly fingers. I was jammed against the table of food with nowhere to go unless I decided to climb onto a plate of tandoori chicken. Utter sacrilege!

"Duck," Rohit whispered as he flicked a chicken leg off his plate and dived after it. I followed his lead.

Ignoring Jabba's sister's calls, we crawled under the table, emerged on the other side, and escaped to a safe corner with our plates to watch the engagement ceremony. It was completed with an exchange of rings and other token items. For a moment the crowd was one as they showered the couple with their blessings.

Soon after, Nisha and Sanjay made their way around the hall, greeting the guests. She was amazing up close and I gaped at her, forgetting to chew.

"Shut your mouth," said Rohit, nudging me. "No one wants to see your half-chewed food."

"She looks awesome," I said.

"Hmmmm."

I swallowed, and clicked a ton of pictures as the couple

approached, focusing mainly on Nisha. Her hands and fore-arms were decorated with the most intricate drawings in a rich brown ink that Rohit explained was henna. There were pictures of mangoes, birds, almonds, and leaves all the way up to her elbows.

She came up to us. "Enjoying yourselves?" she asked in a soft, melodious voice.

"Yeah . . . not bad," I stammered. "I mean, it's awesome and thanks for having me. I've never been to an Indian wedding before so I hope you don't mind me taking pictures."

She laughed. "You're welcome and no, I don't mind, as long as you put only the best ones online. Okay?"

"Deal!" I said. "Not that you could look bad in a single one."

"Your friend is cute, Rohit," she said, giggling.

I could feel my face burning up and I muttered something unintelligible.

"*So* glad you could join us on this auspicious occasion," said Sanjay, looking a little annoyed. "*Chalo*, Nisha. We still have hundreds of people to meet and these new shoes are kill-ing me."

I guessed he must be feeling a little left out and I clicked a couple of pictures of him, too, making a mental note to delete them as soon as I got home.

Nisha sighed. "Getting married is like running a hundred-mile race. Can't wait for the finish line so I can rest. Ta-ta for now," she said. Then she was gone in a swish of gold, her lem-ony perfume still lingering in the air.

"Nisha is the most beautiful woman I've ever seen," I said. "I think I'm in love."

"Don't be stupid," Rohit said. "Girls are the worst."

"Yeah," I said. "You're right." I remembered the girls at Cedarbrae Junior High, who could be just as mean as the boys, sometimes worse. Rohit was right—it was best to keep a safe distance from them at *all* times.

"Let's see if Ma is done paying her respects to Dad's clan so we can head home. The engagement is over so there's no point in hanging around."

I wanted to stay a bit longer but decided to go along with Rohit. After all, he'd been the perfect friend and host these last few days, faithfully sticking to the plan of keeping Mrs. Lal happy.

"'Kay!" I said. "I think I've exhausted the photo ops here." I didn't think a single one I took today would fit the contest theme but at least I had a good collection.

We circled the massive banquet hall, keeping a lookout for Mrs. L. I grabbed a few *gulab jamuns* to sustain me on the journey.

A familiar voice made me freeze midbite, syrup from the sweet trickling down my fingers.

"What rubbish, Mrs. Modi! My brother, Arun, still respects his elder sister. He will do exactly as I say."

Rohit and I exchanged a look, mouthing, *Boa*. She was near us talking to a couple of women. We hid behind a group of men standing beside them and listened.

"Nonsense, Anjali," Mrs. Modi replied. "You'll have to be content being second-best. After marriage a man listens to his wife, not his sister. You should know this by now."

"I'll prove it to you, Mrs. Modi. Stay right here."

We snuck a peek and saw Boa scanning the room. Mrs. Modi, a gargoyle in an orange saree with matching hair, smirked at her companion, a stick-thin lady in a shiny white saree. Without sunglasses, it hurt to look at her for more than a few seconds.

"We better warn Ma—" Rohit started to say when Boa's voice boomed out.

"Priya! Over here. I want a word with you."

"Crap!" I said. "Boa got to her first."

"Shhh," said Rohit.

As soon as Mrs. Lal reached the group, Boa said without preamble, "Priya, did you talk to Arun about Rohit staying back with me?"

"No," said Mrs. Lal, not the slightest tremor in her voice. "I will talk to him when he gets here."

"By that time it'll be too late," said Boa. "I need Arun to bring Rohit's things with him. Not that I can't afford to buy him a whole new wardrobe if need be." This last was directed at her friends. "But I think he might like a few of his own things."

"You're talking as if the decision is yours to make," said Mrs. Lal coldly.

"My money, my rules," said Boa nastily. "I'll call Arun now and settle it. See how simple this is, Mrs. Modi?"

Neither Mrs. Lal nor Rohit uttered a word and my gut clenched. Boa was a venomous viper and needed to be locked up in a tiny cage, *forever.*

Rohit's face was slick with perspiration. "I can't stay here. I won't," he muttered. "I won't let this interfering cow ruin my life. She can't bully us even if she is helping us financially. It's so wrong."

I felt sorry for him. Really sorry. How *whacko* was it to think you were coming to India for a visit and then get forced to stay for the next six years?

"Don't panic," I said. "Your mom will never agree. She hates Boa even more than you do. She'll stand up to her, you'll see."

"It didn't work," Rohit muttered, holding his head in his hands. "Your *stupid* plan didn't work. You were only saying it so you could stay on and take pictures for your *lousy* competition."

"Hey, now hold on a minute!" I said, starting to get annoyed. "We both agreed my way was better. Your way would have just made Boa more determined to keep you here. Your mom's been so happy with you these last few days she's been praising you nonstop to anyone who'll listen."

As if on cue, Mrs. Lal echoed my words. "Rohit is extremely well behaved with people he respects *and* who respect him. My son has not only settled down well in the States but he hasn't forgotten his manners or his culture. He stays with me and we can manage very well without your money, Anjali."

"Rubbish!" Boa said, snapping her fingers. "Love has made you blind to what's best for him and I say he stays here. I know my brother will listen to *me*." She whipped out her cell phone. I did a quick calculation in my head to figure out the time in New York. It was early morning there and she was sure to get ahold of Rohit's dad right away. *Double crap.*

"I have to do something," Rohit said, realizing the same thing. His eyes were wild and panicked. "Now!"

"Relax, Ro. Let's go home and talk this over—"

"Forget it," said Rohit. "Dad will never stand up to Bua. She's too bossy. I'm finished!"

"I'll call Arun and tell him to bring the rest of Rohit's things with him," Boa said, thumbing buttons on her cell phone. "Whatever he can't carry, I'll buy from here. My nephew will have the best education ever! Harvard and Yale will be begging him to enroll after he finishes school."

"Anjali, don't you dare!" said Mrs. Lal, her voice like shards of glass. "You have no right."

"Try and stop me," Boa said and deliberately turned her back on Mrs. Lal.

My jaw dropped and stayed there. How could someone be so mean and cruel to her own family? She truly was the most horrible person ever. Worse than the White Witch.

"That's it," said Rohit. "Time to act."

"What are you going to do?" I asked. "Talk to me, Ro!"

"I know exactly what will work," he said. He walked unsteadily to the buffet table with me right behind him. My stomach oozed into my toes as I saw him mix the red and green chutneys into a bowl, and before I could stop him, he drank all of it. He looked like Harry did in *The Chamber of Secrets* when he had to take Skele-Gro—totally grossed out.

"You okay?" I said, staring at him. "That was really stupid, Ro."

"I've only started," he said, beginning to sweat. He undid the top two buttons of his shirt, taking deep, ragged breaths. He looked green but he was smiling. It reminded me of the crazy, evil grin plastered across Gollum's face every time he looked at the One Ring.

"That stuff inside you can't be good," I said, worried about the allergic reaction he'd mentioned earlier. "You look terrible, bro."

"Chill," said Rohit. "It's all coming out now."

Before I could decipher what he meant, he strode over to Boa and threw up all over her green silk saree.

SEVEN

For a minute Boa stared at Rohit. Then her eyes shifted to Mrs. Lal and finally came to rest on me. I could feel her wrath building up, like a volcano about to erupt. A sour smell hung in the air.

Mrs. Modi came to the rescue. "Poor, *poor* boy," she said, rushing over to him. "Anjali, you scared this child so much, he threw up. Shame on you! Are you all right, Rohit?"

A white-faced Boa glanced around her as people started to pay attention to what was happening. I knew she was dying to spit out some venomous words at the Lals but fear for her reputation kept her silent.

"Rohit, are you all right?" Mrs. Lal said.

He nodded weakly.

All eyes were on Boa, who was jiggling and shaking. Two blobs of vomit fell on the carpet and the crowd moved back, screwing up their noses. I surreptitiously took a couple of pictures of Boa covered in vomit. These would look great online.

Mrs. Lal grabbed a napkin from a guest and started to wipe the barf off Boa but only succeeded in smearing it more thoroughly into her clothes. "You brought this on yourself, Anjali," she said quietly.

"Leave me alone," Boa muttered. "Has anyone seen my phone?"

Mrs. Lal dropped the napkin and went over to Rohit. "Do you need a doctor, *Beta*? Was it something you ate?"

"I-I can't remember," he said.

Someone got a chair and a glass of water and made him sit down. There was a lot of fussing going on and Rohit seemed to be calming down, though he still looked pale and sweaty. Boa was completely forgotten.

Someone dragged me aside. "What did he eat, Dylan, and don't even think of lying to me." I stared into the determined face of Mrs. Lal.

"I-I can't remember," I said, echoing Rohit from a few moments ago.

"Tell me," said Mrs. Lal. "*Now*, Dylan."

I glanced over at my *idiot* of a friend. Why hadn't he thought this through instead of reacting? And what if all that chutney in his system was doing something weird to him right this minute? I'd heard of people dying from peanut allergies. If I didn't tell his mom the truth and Rohit died from a chutney allergy, I'd never forgive myself. But if I did, Rohit would think I'd betrayed him. I'd have to do this quickly and quietly.

"He drank a bowl of chutney, Mrs. L," I whispered. "The red and green ones mixed together."

"Chutney always makes him vomit," exclaimed Mrs. Lal.

"So, this was deliberate," said Boa quietly. "Mother and son conspired to embarrass me in public." The snake had slithered in quietly and eavesdropped on our conversation. Crap! There was nothing I could do about it. Or was there?

While Boa berated her sister-in-law in sibilant whispers, I switched on my camera and started recording a video clip. Boa picked up steam when she realized she could play the victim angle and get the crowd's sympathy so they would forget she was still covered in barf and stank.

"Whoever heard of an *Indian* with a chutney allergy?" bellowed Boa. "He did this to embarrass me. I'm so glad my brother isn't here to witness how badly behaved his child is. You've done a terrible job, Priya. Shame on you!"

"Shut up!" snapped Rohit. "Don't you dare insult Ma."

Mrs. Lal slapped Rohit. "I've had just about enough of you and your disrespectful ways."

The slap echoed in the silent room. I felt so bad for Rohit. No matter how mad Mom might be at me, she'd never embarrass me in public like this or hit me. Rohit's eyes were burning as he looked at his mom and then at Boa.

"Rohit, you will come here and apologize right now," said Boa. "There's no doubt in my mind that you need a strong hand to guide you, so you're definitely not going back to America. *That is final.*"

In a million years I couldn't see Rohit obeying her. I was shocked when he walked up to Boa and stared her in the face. Then he leaned forward and barfed the rest of his dinner all over her gold satin slippers.

EIGHT

A SCORCHING DAY DAWNED AND THE TEMPERA-
ture hovered at 104 degrees. I was too hot to do anything
but lie on the cool tiled floor and watch TV. Mrs. Lal brought
us tall glasses of watermelon juice. I gulped mine down, wondering if she would balk if I asked for a bucket of it with a
straw.

Mother and son had barely exchanged any words since the
barfing episode. Boa had been surprisingly silent, though I'd
seen Mrs. Lal start every time the phone rang. Mr. Lal had
called once to speak to his wife and she'd seemed quite calm
after she hung up. But I couldn't stop wondering what evil
stuff Boa might have said to Mr. Lal. I guessed we'd have to
wait to find out.

Rohit alternated between angry and sulky. Somehow I was
included in the I'm-not-talking-to-you category. He blamed
me for the play-nice plan backfiring (which was totally unfair)
when his get-out-of-India plan would have worked better. He
also said I should have kept my mouth shut at the party and
stayed out of it. I had tried to explain that it was because I was

worried about him that I'd told his mom the truth about his barfing. *I* couldn't lie to Mrs. Lal even if *he* could. It made no difference and an uneasy silence descended on the flat. Even looking through my collection of pictures was no fun. I missed Ro peering over my shoulder, giving me his mostly useless suggestions.

Note to Self: I did what I had to do. Rohit will just have to live with it. The problem was—so would I.

"Deolali is the answer," Mrs. Lal announced after an hour of gloomy silence. "I'm not even sure we should attend the wedding after this fiasco. Bua is sure to throw her money in our faces again." She sighed deeply.

I stared at her, wondering where and what in the world a Deo-lolly was. An edible deodorant stick? I didn't like the sound of it. At all.

"Will we be able to manage if she . . . Bua acts on her threat?" asked Rohit in a small voice.

I knew exactly what he meant. It struck me then, money was so important when you didn't have much. I'd taken it for granted—the food I ate, the house I lived in, and all the luxuries I enjoyed, without thinking about where it was coming from.

"That is for your father and me to worry about, Rohit. Not you," said Mrs. Lal. But from her tone it was evident that she had already started.

"Why don't we just go back home and sort it out?" said Rohit. "I don't want to go to Deolali."

"Because your father would like to see his family even if you don't want to see them. He's worked hard these past few months and needs a break, too. Are you too selfish to see that?"

Rohit looked ashamed as he fiddled with the TV remote. "I'm sorry, Ma," he whispered. "But you should have told me about Bua's threat the day she mentioned it. Instead I had to rely on Dylan to tell me. And you slapped me in front of everyone." His voice wobbled. "How could you embarrass me like that?"

After the Barfing Incident, we'd all come clean. Me about eavesdropping, Mrs. Lal about Bua's threat, and Rohit about deliberately wanting to embarrass Bua so she would leave him alone.

"I'm sorry about that, Rohit, but you did precisely what I asked you not to." Mrs. Lal rubbed her temples wearily. "We're leaving for Deolali tomorrow morning. I'll ask your father to join us there. Then we'll decide what to do about Bua. I don't want to talk about it now." Dark shadows under her eyes were a dead giveaway that she hadn't been sleeping well. I guess this trip wasn't turning out the way any of us had expected.

"Er, Mrs. L," I said. "What's this Deo-lolly?"

Since he was alternating between sarcasm and silence, I knew Rohit wouldn't give me the time of day, let alone answer my question.

Mrs. Lal had started to walk away but stopped and turned around. "It's a small town in the Nashik district. We bought a flat there years ago as a vacation home. We barely go there anymore and we're planning on selling it. I think this may be the last time we'll be visiting."

"Sounds neat, Mrs. L!" I said, relieved that at least she was speaking to me. "I can't wait to explore."

Mrs. Lal looked at me absently, pinching her lower lip. "I hope nothing's been stolen. It's been so *long* since we visited. Thieves cannot resist an empty flat and ours is vacant most of the time."

"Do you have anything valuable there?" I asked.

"Not really. It's quite small and rustic," she said, looking straight at me. "None of the luxuries you're used to back home, Dylan. Not even the amenities you see in *this* flat. Rohit will fill you in."

"I don't mind at all, Mrs. L. I'm a tough guy, not your average American. How bad can it be?" I asked, glancing at Rohit.

Rohit gave me the Gollum smile. "Not too bad at all, my *precious.*"

That should have been my clue, the red flag, to dig a little deeper and ask if *everything* we needed was available there.

· · · · · ·

The next morning a screaming alarm clock woke us up at 5 a.m. Mrs. Lal gave us cups of cold milk and urged us to get dressed quickly. I did everything on autopilot, hoping I'd remembered to put on all the *important* bits of clothing.

The air was warm and sticky when we stepped out of the flat with a backpack each. Mrs. Lal carried a small cooler with snacks and drinks. My camera was slung around my neck, though my eyes were way too blurry to focus enough to take a decent picture. Mrs. Lal had warned us to travel light and wear comfortable clothes. Rohit and I were in shorts and T-shirts but I was already sweaty and in desperate need of a second shower.

We walked to the main road and hailed a cab. "So, are we going to the airport to catch a domestic flight to Lolly?" I asked, yawning behind my hand.

Rohit sniggered. "It's *Deolali*. And if you want to fly there I suggest a large bowl of kidney beans."

"Rohit!" said Mrs. Lal. "There is no need to be so disgusting."

I laughed. "That was a good one. Definitely worth looking into as a future source of energy."

Mrs. Lal gave me the eye and I shut up. While she never really scolded me the way she did Rohit, I knew I couldn't test her patience indefinitely.

"We're going by train and it won't be fun," said Rohit glumly.

"VT station," Mrs. Lal said to the cabdriver. "Open up your dicky, please."

I stared at her in horror. Neither Rohit nor the driver looked fazed. The driver stepped out of the cab. I squinched my eyes shut as I tried to figure out the link between this odd request and a drive to the station. There was a sharp jab in my ribs.

"Dylan?" said Rohit. "Fallen asleep on your feet or what?"

I opened my eyes. The trunk of the cab was open. Rohit's and Mrs. Lal's backpacks were already in there alongside the cooler.

"This is the . . . dicky," I said, hoping Rohit wouldn't guess what I was *really* thinking about and tell his mom. That would be way too embarrassing.

"Bravo," said Rohit as he studied my face. "Can you hurry up?"

I threw my backpack in, thankful I hadn't blurted out a dumb question. Back home, asking a cabbie to show me his dicky would have gotten me into major trouble.

• • • • • •

We zoomed through the streets of the city as it stirred to life. In front of dilapidated huts, made entirely of recyclable material, stoves were already lit, heating up steaming pots of food. Women squatted on sidewalks, totally at home in this open-air kitchen. I was amazed at how comfortable they looked, living on the street. Sufficiently awake by now, I started clicking away on my Nikon, pausing every few seconds to wipe my sweaty hands on my shorts.

Shortly after, we arrived at Victoria Terminus. It was the equivalent of Grand Central Station in New York City, but it couldn't have been *more* different. Nothing had prepared me for the explosion of sight, sound, and color. Even at 6:45 the place was packed. People jostled us, calling out to one another as they hurried toward the dusty white-and-blue carriages waiting patiently along the length of the station. Sweating porters with unimaginably heavy loads balanced on their heads loped by. They were followed by families probably on their way to the country for vacations. The pungent smells of samosas, fresh ink, and pee lingered in the air. I stood there and gaped, enveloped in a frenzy of human activity unlike anything I'd seen before. There also lingered a twinge of panic. If I got lost here, how would I find my way back home? Why had I refused to carry the cell phone Mom had offered? I wrestled my panic into a box and locked it.

"Come along, Dylan," said Mrs. Lal. "You can take pictures once we have found our seats." She expertly navigated through the dense crowds. I was elbowed, shoved, and pinched as we made our way to the very end of the train. By the time we reached our compartment ten minutes later, I was exhausted, sweaty, and ravenous.

"Stinking crowds," Rohit muttered under his breath. He clutched his backpack to his chest, blinking furiously. "*This* is why I *hate* traveling by train out here."

"It's like Grand Central on steroids," I replied, feeling like a lone deer in a herd of migrating wildebeests. I hoped this trip would clear up the air so things could go back to normal between us.

We boarded the Panchvati Express, a superfast train that

connected Mumbai and Nashik, and stepped into its vibrating bowels, which smelled of hot metal and sweat. We passed by the bathroom, and even though the door was closed, I wrinkled my nose involuntarily.

Mrs. Lal saw my expression and patted me on the back. "Don't worry, *Beta*. It's just a three-hour journey. Hopefully you won't have to use the toilet at all."

"I hope so, too," I replied and meant it. I was prepared to steal a diaper before I had to use a bathroom that reeked so badly at the *beginning* of the journey. I prayed someone would come by to clean it soon.

"Told you it wasn't a fun ride," said Rohit, looking equally pained. "Never liked train bathrooms."

"Only if we have to *go*," I said. "I'm going to hold on till we reach Lolly."

A mysterious smile from Rohit again and I knew he was hiding something. Something that had to do with me. I got that he was worried about Boa, and was mad at me, but I wasn't *entirely* to blame for what was happening. He didn't have to be so mean.

"We gotta talk, Ro," I said softly, following Mrs. Lal down the narrow corridor as she searched for our seats. "You can't keep behaving like a jerk for the rest of the trip. I prefer Frodo to Draco Malfoy."

He gave me a brief glance sans smile. "Save your breath, *traitor*. I know what you're going to say and it won't help."

I stared at the back of his head, at the mug-handle ears and the scrawny neck. I was angry, and sorry we were missing out on having fun because of that one incident. But fighting wasn't going to solve anything. If only we could talk, I was sure we'd be able to work this out and save the rest of the trip.

Maybe telling him about my situation would make him realize that I was going through a tough time, too. But every time I decided to come clean, a golf ball would materialize in my throat, choking off the words.

We finally found our "seats," which were actually hard wooden benches with no cushions. I grabbed one by the window. With bars across them, it felt like I was in a cage. Rohit took the window seat opposite me and Mrs. Lal settled herself next to him. She explained that even though seat numbers were assigned, no one really bothered with them as long as you were in the right compartment. It was a first-come, first-grab situation. Overhead a grimy fan whirred, emitting more noise than cool air. I braced myself for a journey that was sure to be *interesting*.

As soon as hawkers saw my pale face peering out the window, they converged on me. Plastic swords, fake watches, umbrellas, hot tea, and samosas were shoved at me. It got hotter as the compartment started to fill up. My thighs were slick against the wooden bench. I fanned myself with a tattered copy of *The Lord of the Rings*, willing the train to move before the flesh melted off my bones.

"Sorry, Dylan," said Mrs. Lal. "This is a short trip and I saw no reason to waste money on an air-conditioned compartment. I hope you do not mind too much?" She'd turned a little pink. I immediately put the book away. I could melt a little to avoid making her feel guilty. Money was going to be tight for them in the next few months and I didn't want to make things worse.

"We're cool, Mrs. L. I'm sure it'll get better when the train starts moving. Right?"

Rohit snorted and I resisted the urge to smack him. Mrs. Lal sighed and looked out the window.

Finally, after an unintelligible squawk of an announcement, the train rumbled to life and slid out of the station. A faint breeze wafted into the compartment, bringing with it the scent of dust, diesel, and boiled rice. I peered through the bars, eager to see more of the legendary Mumbai.

"Ro, look! There's a cat chasing a dog! Never seen that in New York. Have you?"

"Whatever," said Rohit. He stuck in earbuds and leaned back, closing his eyes. "Wake me up when we get there."

And just like that, he'd switched off.

"He's not a morning person," said Mrs. Lal. "Just let him be."

From the way he'd behaved in the last couple of days, he didn't seem to be an afternoon, evening, or night person either but I decided not to bring it up. I was sure I'd find a way to get Rohit alone and really talk things over with him. I had to convince him that Sam was on Frodo's side and always had been. He seemed to have forgotten.

Mumbai slid by in slow motion: shanties built entirely of cardboard boxes and plastic, a jungle of TV antennas pointing steel fingers at the sky, dull gray smoke rising from cooking fires, and rivers of dirty water running between the huts. The slums stood out starkly against a backdrop of high-rises, their windows glinting in the morning sun. I snapped furiously, trying to capture the moment in all its beauty and squalor.

"So what do you think of Mumbai so far?" asked Mrs. Lal. She tucked her feet under herself and poured a cup of tea from the thermos. "Would you like some?" she asked, holding it out to me. She seemed more relaxed the farther we sped from the city and I hoped it would be the same for Rohit.

"More people than I'd ever imagined," I said, my eyes roving through the packed compartment. "And no tea for me, thanks." The thought of having to use the disgusting bathroom kept me from having anything to eat or drink even though my stomach rumbled ominously.

Mrs. Lal smiled. "Yes, India's population is currently over a billion. The average Indian goes through a lot just to survive out here. In the West people take their comfortable lives for granted and complain a lot. If they had to spend a month in India during the summer, they'd realize just how lucky they are. One should always appreciate what one has because it could be gone in a moment."

I studied her face. Did she think *I* was spoiled and didn't appreciate what life had doled out to me? Was this what Dad had been trying to tell me, in his own way?

Mrs. Lal sipped her tea, glancing at Rohit before staring out the window, a faraway expression on her face. I realized then how disappointed she was with him. At the moment, said subject of our thoughts was tapping his foot in time to the music, totally oblivious.

"I'm sure Rohit appreciates everything you've done for him," I said. "But I think he'd be happiest with his family, no matter what the lifestyle." There, I'd said it and I hoped Mrs. Lal wouldn't get mad at me for interfering.

She gave me a small, sad smile. "You're a loyal friend to my Rohit. He was lonely till he met you. I know you will miss him if he stays here, but his father and I have to make some very tough decisions. It's not easy to live in New York without a decent income. It might even mean we all have to come back to Mumbai."

No!

Till I'd met Rohit, I'd been miserable, too. Sucking at sports, being clumsy, and being a fantasy nerd somehow sealed my fate as a lone loser. I had to make sure Rohit came back with me. He was my only friend!

Mrs. Lal leaned forward and patted my knee. "If there is anything you want to talk about, don't hesitate." Her eyes gazed into mine. How could she tell something was bothering me? I couldn't even talk to Ro, so there was no way I'd take her up on the offer.

"Sure, Mrs. L. Thanks."

Crammed onto the bench beside me was a couple with six kids. One of them stood in front of me, gaping.

"Hey!" I said, smiling.

The boy ran and hid his face in his mother's lap where another kid was already sitting. A baby was cradled in her arms, sucking noisily at a plastic bottle filled with milk.

About half an hour into the journey, the woman next to me put her kid on the seat and took off to the bathroom. The boy who'd been staring at me came over, climbed onto my lap, and said, "I'm Chottu."

"I'm Dylan. You want to play?" I asked.

He nodded.

"Okay, know how to arm wrestle?"

He stared at me blankly.

I made him sit beside me and grabbed his hand, our elbows firm on the seat. By way of miming, I explained the rules. Chottu grinned and nodded. We went a couple of rounds where I grunted exaggeratedly while the little shrimp pushed my arm down to the seat with both of his, giggling excitedly.

"Dylan, be careful," said Mrs. Lal. "It's not a good idea to play with a stranger's kid without their permission. They can get touchy."

The other passengers were watching, clapping and encouraging Chottu, who was having a great time. "Don't worry, Mrs. L—" I started to say when two things happened at once.

I felt a tickling sensation on my ankle and looked down to see a large cockroach trekking up my leg. I choked back a yell of disgust. I forgot I was still holding on to Chottu's hand and flailed my arms and legs so hard, I flung him off the seat. Chottu landed on the floor just as his mom returned.

The minute she saw him fall she screeched, putting Hedwig to shame.

"Why you touch my child?" she yelled. "You hurt him, you *gora*? Bad boy!"

"I'm sorry, really sorry. We were just playing and then this cockroach distracted me," I explained as I tried to help Chottu up.

But he was bawling—probably from the shock of falling, since he *looked* fine—which set his mom off even more. It took fifteen minutes of cajoling by Mrs. Lal to calm down Chottu's mom. A chocolate cake changed hands, too, before things got quiet again.

"Kids are off-limits, Dylan," said Mrs. Lal grimly. "Don't even *look* in their direction. Understood?"

"Sorry, Mrs. L."

Rohit had watched the whole fiasco but hadn't said a word. He shook his head and closed his eyes. He would have had my back if we were home. I decided to listen to music and dozed off.

· · · · · ·

I jerked awake to loud clapping and the sight of three very masculine-looking women invading our compartment. They wore colorful sarees, garish makeup, and lots of glass bangles that clinked on their hairy arms. Who were they? *What* were they?

"Paisa de Baba, paisa dey do," the tallest woman sang in a scratchy voice.

She strode over and pinched my cheek. Then, smiling menacingly, she stuck her palm under my nose, begging for money. She reeked of sour sweat and a cloyingly sweet perfume. I almost gagged.

I slapped her hand away. The smile vanished. She called out in Hindi to her companions, who were busy harassing other passengers. They immediately made their way over to me, eyeing me like a tasty tidbit. My pulse raced.

"What . . . do you want?" I asked, trying not to squeak.

"Money," one replied, in a guttural voice. "Or you will have too much bad luck."

"Thanks, but I have plenty of that without your help," I said.

Mrs. Lal took out a ten-rupee note and shoved it into the hands of the nearest woman. "Take this," she said sternly, "and please leave us alone." She added something in Hindi but her tone said it all.

Rohit had pulled out his earbuds and was leaning forward, glaring at the trio. Mrs. Lal put a hand on his knee and he sat back, glancing at me, his eyebrows raised. I nodded imperceptibly to let him know I was okay. I was glad he finally cared.

The tall woman scratched the two-day stubble on her square jaw, clapped rudely in Mrs. Lal's face, and walked away. Most of the other passengers took out various denominations of rupees and pushed them into the women's callused hands.

I was seething with anger and, if I was honest, fear, too. "Super-aggressive beggars! Why do you encourage them?" I said.

"Shhhh," said Rohit, rolling his eyes. "They're eunuchs called *hijdas* here."

I scrubbed the spot where the eunuch had touched me. "Go on," I said.

"No one argues with *hijdas*," Rohit explained. "Easier to give them what they want."

"Why?"

"Because they'll abuse and curse you. Most people in India are superstitious. To be cursed by a *hijda* is bad luck. And if they bless you . . . you have a run of good luck."

I thought of Mom then, and the laughing Buddha keychain she took with her everywhere—a gift from her college roomie from Nepal. She would have *everyone* hunting for it on the rare occasions she misplaced it. In some ways, people were pretty similar the world over. Sometimes it was best to go with the flow.

"Wait!" I called out to a departing *hijda*.

She turned. I took out a fifty-rupee note and gave it to her. "I need luck. Lots of it."

She smiled and plucked the note out of my fingers. Then she placed a hand on my head and murmured something, her eyes closed.

"All will be well," she said. Then she winked at me and sashayed toward the next compartment. The passengers squeezed back, giving her a wide berth.

"That was a lot of money, Dylan," said Mrs. Lal. "Why?"

"While in India . . ." I said, hoping she wouldn't question me too closely.

"All right. But don't encourage any more beggars or word will spread and we'll have a stampede here."

"Just this once," I replied, hoping I'd been blessed with enough luck to stop whatever was happening with my parents a million miles away.

With a lot left over to bring my friend back home with me.

NINE

THE PRESSURE ON MY BLADDER WAS GETTING WORSE even though I'd barely taken a couple of sips of water all morning. "I need to go to the bathroom," I muttered, nudging Rohit with my foot. He'd put away his iPod a while ago and was gazing at the dusty landscape whizzing past.

"Don't even *think* about it," he said with a frown. "You have to hold on."

"I'm in pain, Ro!"

Rohit shrugged. "Trust me on this one. You *don't* want to go."

"I'm not sure if you're stopping me just to make me suffer or if it's really that bad."

He tried to swat me and I ducked. Mrs. Lal told us to behave and continued to flip through a magazine. The midday heat made everyone in the compartment drowsy and the noise level had fallen from a deafening roar to a quiet murmur. I was roasting. I wouldn't be able to handle the heat and my bursting bladder much longer. It would be touch and go.

"This heat's killing me, Ma," said Rohit, voicing my thoughts. "Going to Deolali in the peak of summer is a terrible idea."

"We're almost there," Mrs. Lal said calmly. "If anyone has to complain about the heat it should be Dylan and I don't see him whining. Why don't you try to be more like him?"

I hated it when Dad compared me to my athletic cousin (who was really into soccer), telling me to be more like him. From Rohit's scowl I knew she'd hit the wrong nerve, too.

The train clattered on to the steady refrain in my head.

I gotta go pee.

I gotta go pee.

I gotta go pee.

I tried to think of something to distract me. *Jalebis*, samosas, and biryani. The latest photos I'd taken. Winning the competition and proving Dad wrong. Nothing worked. Visions of peeing my pants filled my head. I glanced at my neighbor with the kids, trying to decide if I should ask for a diaper. Desperate situations called for desperate measures. Unfortunately, since the fiasco with Chottu, his mother glared at me suspiciously every time I looked in her direction.

The train started to slow. Relieved, I looked out the window. The sun was high overhead and the station slid into view. Igatpuri—a rural town before Deolali, Mrs. Lal announced—was nestled among green fields and looked like a postcard. In the distance a girl wearing a bright-yellow skirt and top walked gracefully, a pot balanced on her head. It was such a beautiful scene, I had to take a picture. I snapped a couple of frames while my bladder throbbed painfully.

As the train wheezed to a stop, vendors swarmed up. A filthy hand holding a leaf cup filled with little golden balls and chutney parked itself under my nose. They smelled incredible.

"*Aloo vadas*," explained Mrs. Lal, noting my questioning look. "Boiled potatoes mixed with spices, cilantro, and fried in a chickpea batter."

·My stomach growled, my bladder ached, and my throat was parched. I clamped my legs shut and froze in place, not daring to move a muscle. Should I just go to the bathroom and get it over with? A few moments of toilet terror and I'd be a free man—able to breathe, eat, and drink. I decided to give it a few more minutes before making a decision.

Mrs. Lal was still talking. "I'd rather we don't eat anything from here. I don't want you to get Delhi belly. Then you will *have* to use the washroom for number two and it will not be pleasant!"

"What's Delhi belly?" I asked.

"Diarrhea," Rohit piped in.

But we're not *in Delhi,* I wanted to protest. Instead I nodded as the train started up with a deep shudder. "Gently please, *gently*," I muttered under my breath as I clamped my legs tighter, trying not to sob. Rohit seemed to be suffering, too, but he made no attempt to use the train bathroom, either. He looked like someone whose fingernails were being ripped out, one at a time.

As the train pulled away from Igatpuri, I saw a little boy peeing against a wall, sunlight glinting on the arc of water as we sped past. That was it. I cursed him silently and stood up.

"I have to go," I announced to no one in particular. "Now."

"All right, Dylan," said Mrs. Lal with a deep sigh as she handed me a wad of tissues. "Try not to touch anything. Do you want Rohit to go with you?"

I took one look at Rohit's mutinous expression and shook my head. Then, stepping over bags, parcels, and sleeping kids scattered through the swaying compartment, I made my way to the bathroom. Even as I approached, the stench stopped me dead in my tracks. I sucked it up and took two more steps. Yellow liquid trickled out from under the door. I moved back in the nick of time. Hobbling like Gimli trailing behind Aragorn and Legolas as they searched for the hobbits, I made it back to my seat and didn't move at all after that. I seriously contemplated stuffing the wad of tissues into my underwear but even for that I'd need privacy.

I softly chanted *What doesn't kill you makes you stronger* the rest of the way.

Thankfully the next stop was Deolali. We gathered our stuff and headed toward the door. I was practically tiptoeing. Sheer willpower was the only thing that stood between me and peeing my pants.

• • • • • •

Deolali was a bustling city compared with Igatpuri but didn't come close to Mumbai when it came to sheer population. Wires crisscrossed the low buildings, as if someone had thrown a huge net from the skies, trapping everyone under it.

The waiting hall and ticket counter looked shabby and badly in need of a fresh coat of paint. People in military-green uniforms waited for the train to stop, while porters watched the compartments go past, their shrewd eyes gauging which passengers had the least luggage and the most money to pay for their services. They were dressed in red kurta-pajamas (what I'd thought were pj's before Rohit enlightened me) with a copper tag bearing a number around their arms.

As soon as we stepped off the train we were surrounded by the gang in red—we qualified for the less-luggage, more-money category. One of them started to tug my backpack off my shoulder.

"HELP!" I yelled. Aggressive beggars on the train and now thieves in the guise of porters. "This man's trying to steal my backpack. LET GO!"

The man tugged harder. "Come, *gora baba*!"

"Ruko!" Rohit called out authoritatively. *"Koi nahi chahiye."* He pushed his glasses up his sweaty nose and waved him off.

The man backed away, scowling.

"Don't worry, Dylan," said Mrs. Lal in a soothing voice.

"They are not trying to steal your belongings; they just want to earn a living."

"And since you looked like a helpless white foreigner . . ." said Rohit with a shrug.

I punched Rohit on his shoulder a little harder than necessary and he winced.

"If I weren't in a bit of a *delicate* situation, I would have carried your bag and mine," I snapped.

"Same for me, dude," he said.

"That's enough, Rohit, Dylan," Mrs. Lal said. "Let's get a scootie. I'm sure we all need to get to a clean toilet, fast."

"Like yesterday," I said.

"You want to try using the one at the station?" Mrs. Lal asked. "It might be better than the one on the train."

The doubt in her voice made me hesitate. I shook my head. I'd made it this far, so I might as well go to the one at the flat.

Deolali was hot and humid. We stepped out of the station to an onslaught of scootie drivers. They tugged and pulled us toward their respective vehicles. Their enthusiasm was overwhelming and frankly exhausting as I clutched my backpack close, hoping that in all this tugging and pulling, the dam wouldn't burst.

"Stay together, boys," Rohit's mom squeaked as she wrestled a bearlike driver who was dragging her to his scootie by the strap of her purse.

"Where you go?" the driver growled. "Come, I take you."

"No, me," roared another. "*I* take you. Very cheap fare."

Rohit scowled as they crowded around us with sweaty faces and bad breath. Suddenly the crowd parted and a buff guy in a blue turban strolled up to us.

"*Namaste, Behenji,*" said the man in a calm voice. "Where would you like to go? It will be my deepest honor to take you to your destination."

"Thank you," said Mrs. Lal, mopping her face with a handkerchief and giving him a tentative smile. "Gurudwara Road, Deolali Camp."

I knew I should probably memorize the address but I figured that as long as I stuck with one of the Lals, I didn't need to.

"Of course. Please to follow this humble driver."

The other drivers swore at him but moved out of the way. Our burly rescuer shot a volley of rude words at them. An answering volley came at him from all directions. He ignored them.

We followed Muscles to his vehicle, which was this awesome three-wheeled yellow scooter covered with a soft black top. It looked like a fat bee on skates. The driver sat up front and there was room for us to squeeze in at the back. A picture of a six-armed woman wearing animal skins was painted on the side. This man sure had an *interesting*-looking girlfriend. As I walked around the back to the other side, I noticed three chilies and a lemon hanging next to the tailpipe. Weird place to keep a snack. This guy definitely had odd tastes. Painted on the back was HORN OK PLEASE. When I looked around, almost every scootie had the same message painted on the rear. I had no idea what that meant, but I guess it explained why people honked all the time.

"Shouldn't we put the luggage in the trunk . . . er, dicky?" I asked, looking at mother and son to see if they were impressed with my fabulous and accurate memory.

"Get in," said Rohit. "There's no dicky in a scootie. Just keep the bag on your lap or wedge it between your feet."

"Okay," I said. I wouldn't have minded balancing the bag on my head if it meant we could get to a clean bathroom faster.

Rohit got in from one side and his mother from the other, sandwiching me in the middle. Rohit jammed his bag between his feet and so did Mrs. Lal. Muscles offered to keep the cooler in front and Mrs. Lal passed it to him. Then Ro and Mrs. L clasped the horizontal bar attached to the back of the driver's seat, bracing themselves.

"Aren't you both forgetting something?" I said, looking smugly from one to the other. I could understand Rohit being careless about rules, but Mrs. Lal? That just wasn't on.

"What?" Rohit replied over the din of Muscles gunning the engine.

"Seat belts," I roared, groping behind my seat.

"There aren't any," yelled Rohit. He grabbed my hand and put it onto the bar. "Why do you think we put you in the middle? Hang on!"

The three-wheeler shot off from the curb and into the midst of the traffic. My bladder gave a warning throb. I clenched my legs and jaw tight as we zigzagged through the narrow lanes, my knuckles white from holding on for dear life. The driver made a sharp turn, flew over a speed bump, and hurtled onto the main road.

Everyone was honking okay, maybe to let people know they were alive and driving. Bells tinkled, bus horns blared, and above it all was the sound of thumping music. The shopkeepers along the main street probably thought it was way too quiet and had decided to raise the noise levels by a few more decibels.

Muscles swerved expertly in and out of the traffic, taking some turns almost on two wheels. We bumped through potholes and were airborne for a few brief seconds before a jarring touchdown. I'm sure a drop or two must have leaked out. It was the most exciting and excruciating ride I've experienced.

We finally hurtled down a side road that was a graveyard compared to the main road. We stopped in front of a squat gray building and got out, shaky and dusty, while Mrs. Lal paid the driver.

"Please call this humble servant if you want a tour of Deolali," he said, pocketing the money and inclining his head. "Ask for Khan and they will tell you where to find me."

He seemed really into himself, but he must have been kinda important since he'd hijacked us from under the other drivers' noses and gotten away with it.

Mrs. Lal nodded. Khan gunned the engine again and shot off, waving goodbye.

The entrance of the three-story building was cool and dark. A flight of stairs faced us. No elevator in sight. "What floor are we on?" I asked, gritting my teeth and pulling my backpack higher on my shoulder. My willpower had weakened considerably during the scootie ride. The dam was about to explode.

"Third," said Mrs. Lal. "I should warn you, the cleaner doesn't start until tomorrow. I will expect both of you to help so we can make it livable by—"

"Bathroom," I said in a strangled yelp, cutting her short. "I'll scrub our flat and the neighbors' flats if you want, Mrs. L, just as soon as I go."

"Almost there, Dylan," she said, patting me on the back. "Be strong."

Rohit climbed at a steady pace. I followed gingerly on tiptoes. I had to avoid peeing my pants because I knew Ro would never let me forget it. I didn't even want to think about what Mom would say when she heard about it, and she would, if I knew Rohit well enough.

Rohit slid the key in and fumbled with the lock while Mrs. Lal caught up. As soon as he flung the door open, she flicked on the switch but no lights came on. The interior was murky, dust motes dancing in the weak sunlight pouring in through closed windows. A musty smell hung in the warm, still air.

"Power outage again!" she sighed. "When will the building management get a generator? We've been asking for years. It's just as well we're planning to sell this place."

"No problem, Mrs. L. Just tell me where to go."

I dumped my backpack on the ground, shuffled into the bathroom, and shut the door. Fingers of pale light slid in through the opaque windows high up on the wall. I scrabbled with the zipper on my shorts. *Just. One. More. Second. Please and thank you!*

My eyes adjusted to the gloom. I looked down and got the shock of my life. There was a white keyhole-shaped depression in the floor. Toward the top was a hole filled with water. A chain, attached to a water tank on the wall, hung three-fourths of the way to the floor. *But the most important bit was missing!*

"Oh crap!" I yelled as I yanked up my shorts, pulled my T-shirt over them, and raced out of the bathroom. Where was the toilet? Who would steal a freaking toilet?

"What?" said Rohit, who'd been splashing his face at the sink just outside.

"*Someone stole your toilet, Ro!* There's just a hole in the ground. What are we going to do?"

Rohit stared at me for a minute. Then he collapsed on the ground, laughing so hard his glasses fell off. I marched back inside, slamming the door behind me. It dawned on me (too late!) that the hole in the ground *was* the toilet. An *Indian* toilet—the first and only one I'd seen on this trip. Now I understood the glint in Rohit's eyes, those mysterious comments, that Gollum-like smile. This is what he'd been supposed to "fill me in" on. And conveniently hadn't.

When I came out a good ten minutes later, weak-kneed with relief, Rohit was in the bedroom, talking to his mother. "Someone stole the toilet!" he shrieked, imitating me. "I will *never* let him forget this . . ."

The flat rang with laughter as Mrs. Lal tried, unsuccessfully, to get him to calm down.

TEN

WHEN I MUSTERED THE COURAGE TO WALK INTO the bedroom, Mrs. Lal was wiping tears from her eyes. "I'm so sorry, Dylan, but I thought you knew about Indian toilets," she said, trying desperately to look serious. She stopped, cleared her throat, and tried to compose herself. The crinkling around her eyes gave her away.

I shifted from one foot to the other. "You'd, er . . . said that you were worried something might be stolen from the flat . . . so I assumed . . ."

Neither of them was buying my lame excuse. How was I supposed to know? I mean, it's the twenty-first century! Ro was definitely not going to let me forget this. The list was growing long. Nothing to do but suck it up.

"Be back in a sec," said Rohit as he raced to use the bathroom, too.

"I'd asked Rohit to tell you about it," Mrs. Lal continued, blushing. "I thought it would be better coming from him than me but it's my fault, too. I should have warned you. We rarely use this place, so it didn't make sense wasting money on upgrading it. Sorry, Dylan." She looked away, blushing some more.

"We're cool, Mrs. L," I said, embarrassed by her apology. "I'll just put it down to a new experience."

"I'll get toilet paper when I go shopping but in the meantime, all you have to remember is to use your left hand to . . . er . . . wash up. *Never* use the right, which is your eating hand. It's culturally and hygienically inappropriate."

I stared at her, feeling the heat creep up my face at hearing detailed instructions about something I barely felt comfortable talking about with a doctor. She was deep into the TMI zone and I wanted her to stop.

"Sure, Mrs. L," I said, wondering if I should ask Rohit for a demo. No way. He'd never let me live it down. *Dylan, my man, you're going to figure out this right-left-hand thing on your own. It isn't rocket science.*

Rohit came back moments later and threw himself on the bed, raising a puff of dust. "I'm tired, Ma. Can we eat first and then clean up?"

"No, Rohit," she said, her voice sharp. "*First* we clean and then we eat. I do not like to sleep in a dusty bed, and nor will you. Stop arguing with me and get to work. You'll thank me later when your stomachs are full and all you want to do is crawl into bed and sleep."

Mrs. Lal handed me a duster. "Get started in the living room with Rohit and I'll do the bedrooms. With all of us working it should be done in no time and then we'll go for a late lunch."

"You're not serious, are you, Mrs. L?" I said. "I'm so weak I can barely walk." I'd avoided eating and drinking completely during the train ride and now I was starving. "It's so hot! Can't we clean up when the power comes back on?"

As if on cue, the fan whirred to life and the fluorescent tube light came on, making the sunlit room brighter. Mrs. Lal winked and draped the duster on my shoulder. "The electricity gods have spoken."

I made one last attempt. "Can't we call a maid service or something?"

"No, we can't," she said firmly. "I've arranged for a cleaning lady to start with us tomorrow but today we're on our own. The sooner we finish, the sooner you eat."

I admired Mrs. L but was annoyed, too. I was tired and hungry. Why couldn't the cleaning wait for the professionals like it would have back home?

New Year's Eve at Chez Moore. The place was swarming with hired help: cleaners, florists, chefs, and servers. Maria was ordering everyone around while Mom was getting dressed. Dad was powering through some final negotiations on a large building deal. He shooed me away when I went into his office to ask if I could borrow the car and driver the next day. I wandered into the kitchen and sampled a few canapés that were being served that night. As soon as I was done, Maria was at my side to whisk away the plate. I strolled out of the kitchen and watched

the frenzied last-minute activity, wishing I could be a part of it.
Weirdly I was hungrier after my snack than before. I went back
into my room, picked up The Hobbit, *and slipped into the Shire.*
Somehow, a hole in the hillside seemed a friendlier place than my
own house.

"All right, Mrs. L," I said, sliding the duster from my shoulder. "We'll do it."

Rohit glowered at her but she'd already turned away and was pulling the dusty sheets off the bed.

"Come on, Ro. You know it's no use arguing with your mom," I said, dragging him away to the living room.

"Stop being such a suck-up," he snapped. "I bet you've never done anything like this in your life!"

"There's always a first time," I said, trying to keep my temper under control. "And really, I don't mind. How hard could it be?"

"Must be such a unique experience for you," Rohit said, an ugly sneer on his face. "Want me to click a few pictures while you're slumming? As a keepsake for your album?"

"What's *wrong* with you?" I snapped, dangerously close to yelling. "Why are you being such a baby?"

"Mom's already mad at me and you're making me look worse by taking her side all the time." He blinked rapidly, arms twitching. "You're supposed to be *my* friend."

"Yeah, but that doesn't mean I have to be a doormat," I said. "You need to lighten up, bro. Your whining is getting really boring. And don't forget the toilet trick you just pulled. I looked like a total dork and I almost peed my pants, but you don't see *me* crying about it!"

For a moment we stood there glaring at each other. After a tentative cease-fire, I didn't want to start fighting again. The last couple of days had been bad enough. Besides, he was all I had, especially with the stuff between my mom and dad. They might not even be living under the same roof when I got back. But I hoped that wouldn't happen. The *hijda*'s blessings might work.

"Okay, listen," I said when Rohit still looked angry a few minutes later. "I'm on your side. Always have been and always will be. But I'm starving. Can we get this done so we can go eat? Your mom's a tough lady and we both know she's not going to budge till she gets her way."

Rohit's puckered face relaxed. "Yeah, that she is. Yours is so laid-back compared to mine. We should switch someday."

"Yeah, someday," I said, trying to ignore the ache in my chest. "So where do we begin?"

The tiny living room had a floral-patterned sofa, a dining table thick with dust pushed against the wall, and four chairs. A hutch containing a few glass knickknacks was the only other piece of furniture. A door led to a small balcony that Rohit and I managed to force open in spite of the rusted hinges.

A light breeze wafted in and hot sunshine speckled the brown-and-white tiled floor. I stepped out. Across the street from our building, green fields stretched out as far as the eye could see. A lone farmer pedaled along a narrow road snaking through the field and the sound of his cycle bell tinkled, soft and sweet in the distance. Mostly there was a buzzing silence—the kind that makes you wonder if you've gone deaf or if your ears are ringing. Despite the heat, I stood there mesmerized.

"We ain't in Kansas anymore, Ro! This is awesome."

"Whatever," he said. But seeing my expression, he added, "Yeah, it's not bad."

We hurried back inside and started thumping the cushions, wiping down the tables and chairs, all the while sneezing and coughing.

"This is *pathetic*," said Rohit, sneezing five times in quick succession, his glasses shooting off his nose with the first violent one. "We could have been at an air-conditioned movie theater back home enjoying a Coke right this minute. But here we are in the middle of nowhere, dusting!" He grabbed his glasses, wiped them, and jammed them back on his nose.

"Yeah, hadn't counted on such strenuous activity," I said. "But once it's done, we can rent bikes and explore Lolly-land tomorrow. I have a feeling I'm going to get some great shots. What say?"

"Maybe," said Rohit. He was red-faced, sweating, and definitely not having a good time. I was feeling grimy and hungrier than before. I would have traded my pinkie for a shower and a snack but I wasn't going to buckle before he did. After all, Sam was the tough one, not Frodo.

Time crawled on as we swept tons of dust, a couple of dead lizards, and a petrified mouse into large garbage bags. Finally Mrs. Lal walked in to check our progress, a cobweb floating from the tip of her nose. "I'm done with the bedrooms. I could give you boys a hand in here. Then we freshen up and head out for lunch. Okay?"

"Now you're talking," I said, nodding my head vigorously. I was so hungry, I was ready to start gnawing on my fingers . . . or Rohit's.

"Thanks, Ma," said Rohit, surprising us both with his sudden mood swing as he started mopping the floor. Within half an hour the room was clean. With the balcony door open and the fan at full speed, the intense heat was bearable.

"Good work, boys," said Mrs. Lal. "You can stop now."

I almost sank to my knees and kissed her feet.

"Go freshen up while I clean the kitchen." She wiped a hand across her sweaty forehead, leaving a black smear of dust.

"I'll go first," said Rohit. He whooshed past, stripping off his T-shirt and exposing a rib cage that belonged in an anatomy textbook. I promised myself I was going to get in a lot more exercise in Lolly-land no matter how hot the weather. I was going to get fit even if it killed me!

"Can I help in the kitchen, Mrs. L?" I asked, hoping she wouldn't take me up on the offer.

"That's sweet, Dylan. Thank you, but no," she replied. "There's some lemonade in a thermos," she said, pointing to the cooler that was still by the front door. "Help yourself."

Rummaging through the cooler I found some granola bars and the thermos. Armed with a cup of lemonade and an almond-honey bar, I headed to the balcony. It was late afternoon and in the scorching heat very little stirred. Bees droned close by and the whispering of the wind through the trees was soothing. This was quickly becoming my favorite place in the flat.

The tinkling of a bell caught my attention. A man with a bright-blue box, fitted with wheels and attached to the front of his cycle, came into view. Along one side of the box was a row of bottles with colorful liquids. The sign on the box read MITHU'S GOLA in fancy writing. What was a *gola*? I watched in anticipation of discovering another exotic food I could introduce to my stomach.

As soon as he stopped and rang the bell again, children from nearby homes and flats swarmed into the street. They crowded round him, all talking at once. The man opened the lid of the box. I leaned forward and watched him take out a chunk of ice from what turned out to be a freezer. He wrapped a brown rag around it and shaved it on a blade fitted on the lid. He held his hand below the blade to collect the ice shavings and then when he had enough, he shaped it into a ball and stuck a wooden stick into its center. No gloves. Bare hands with dirty fingernails. No one seemed to notice or care. Mithu, which I assumed was his name since it was painted on his freezer, asked the kid he was serving a question.

"Lal!" I heard her shriek and she pointed to a bottle.

Even as she pointed, I knew she'd said *red*. Rohit had told me what his last name meant.

Mithu lifted up the bottle and shook it over the ice, turning it over and over. The ice turned a bright red, like blood on snow, and he handed it to her. She paid him and then, slurping greedily, she walked away.

The man started making the next *gola*, which I now realized was the Indian version of a snow cone. He made a few more and then trundled off, ringing his bell. With deep regret I realized I'd forgotten to take pictures. My camera was still in the bedroom. I made a mental note to keep it around my neck at all times. Except when I was in the bathroom, though I did plan on taking a few pictures of the toilet when no one was around. Mom would love to see what I'd experienced. Dad, too. He'd never again say that I was so spoiled, I couldn't rough it or adapt to a situation.

Rohit came out just then, toweling his hair dry. "Your turn, and hustle. I'm starving," he said.

I gulped the last of my warm lemonade and headed inside.

"Use the cold-water tap," Rohit yelled out behind me. "Don't even think of turning on the hot water."

"'Kay," I yelled back. "I'd prefer a cold shower anyway."

As soon as I turned on the tap, I understood why Ro had warned me. The water from the cold-water tap was hot. I would have been poached if I'd turned on the hot water! I shampooed and scrubbed, feeling the sweat and grime melt away. I was even hungrier now that I was clean.

"I won't take long, boys," said Mrs. Lal, diving into the bathroom the minute I stepped out.

True to her word, she was done in ten minutes and we headed out for lunch. I could have eaten a cow, but knew better than to say it out loud.

ELEVEN

WOULD YOU LIKE TO TRY SOUTH INDIAN FOOD, Dylan?" Mrs. Lal asked as we walked along the main street.

"I'm so hungry, Mrs. L, I'll eat anything."

After a brisk ten-minute walk, we came to a restaurant called Sagar. Nothing about the place seemed old or sagging. The name was plastered on a board above the entrance and decorated with garlands made of orange flowers. It was spelled out in English lettering and a squiggly font. People crowded the sidewalk outside and spilled over onto the road, chattering loudly. "What's with the name?" I asked.

"It means 'ocean' in Hindi. I guess because tides of people flow in and out of this place during the day," said Mrs. Lal. "It has the best *idlis* and *dosas* in all of Deolali, and is worth the short wait."

Rohit and I groaned out loud.

"I don't want to wait, Ma. I'll drop dead."

I nodded, pointing at Rohit. "What he said!"

A tall man with greasy hair, wearing a tight-fitting black vest and tighter pants, came up to us. "How many pliss?" he said in a hissy whisper.

"Three," Mrs. Lal said. "How much time before we get a table? The boys are very hungry. If it's going to take long, we will go elsewhere."

He scanned the crowd near the entrance and kneaded his forehead with a theatrical air. I had a feeling he had done this loads of times before.

"Pliss to understand, madam, this very busy time. But for you"—he checked his watch, frowning—"thirteen and a half minutes."

"And if it's more than that, is our lunch free?" I asked.

The man inserted his pinkie into his ear, shook it vigorously, pulled it out, and took a sniff. "Funny bwoay! Nothing in India is free." I hoped he stayed *far* away from the kitchen.

"Thirteen and a half minutes," said Rohit. "Whoever heard of a wait time like that?"

"What a weirdo!" I said, counting down the minutes in my mind. "I'm sure he's lying. It'll be half an hour *at least* and by that time I'll be dead."

Mrs. Lal leaned against a wall at the side of the entrance. "Wait and see. They're quite accurate."

In ten minutes we were seated. A boy who looked a little smaller than Ro, dressed in frayed shorts and a white shirt, came to take our order. I watched him in surprise. I'd never seen servers this young in a restaurant before. You have to be at least fourteen in New York to work. Dad may be on my case about some things, but at least I didn't have to have a job.

Note to Self: Be thankful you don't have to earn a living yet!

"What would you like to try, Dylan?" Mrs. Lal asked as we all studied the single-page menu.

"Try the plain *dosa* with coconut chutney and *sambar*," said Rohit. "You'll like it."

"What's sam-ba, Mrs. L?" I wasn't about to forget the toilet trick he'd pulled. I'd decided it would be safer to double-check with Mrs. Lal in case he was planning on tricking me again by suggesting something gross.

"What's the matter with you?" said Rohit, frowning.

"No offense, but I don't feel like being the butt of another joke. You've been kind of whack-a-doodle on this trip. I'd rather be safe than sorry."

"Whatever," said Rohit, his voice cold. "There goes a *dosa*, just behind you."

I turned to look, feeling like crap for dissing my best bud in front of his mom. But it was hard to forget how he'd rolled on the ground laughing at me just a few hours ago. I wasn't going to give him another chance to embarrass me, especially in a packed restaurant.

A huge golden wafer folded in half seemed to float past, bigger than the tray it was on. Only skilled maneuvering enabled the waiter to carry it to the table without bumping into anyone and shattering it.

"Is that it, Mrs. L?" I asked to make sure I wouldn't end up ordering fried snakes or monkey brains. I'm always up for trying something new, but that's not what I was in the mood for right now.

"Rohit's right, Dylan," she said, smiling. "And by the way, this is a vegetarian restaurant so no matter what you order, you can't go wrong."

I was seriously beginning to think she was a mind reader. Her mom-antenna was always up and alert. Rohit wouldn't be able to keep a secret from her for long. Not a good thing most of the time. In contrast, my mom mostly left me alone unless I wanted to talk to her, and then she did try to listen. Mom came out way ahead in that respect.

It was weird how I kept making these comparisons between Mrs. L and Mom. And even though Rohit's mom was cool, spending so much time with her made me realize how much I liked mine. I missed Mom more than ever.

"Yep," I said. "I'll try a do-sa with some sam-ba."

Rohit ordered *idlis* and his mother ordered a *thali*. Everything looked so unusual, I had to take pictures. At first I stuck to taking pictures of the food going by our table. I stood up and took shots of the dishes served to other people in the restaurant. Mrs. Lal asked me to sit down but I was having too good a time to stop. Encouraged by the other patrons who were grinning and hamming it up for the camera, I walked around taking close-ups of them eating an array of colorful foods. I even asked our kid server to pose for me and he smiled willingly.

Someone tapped me on the shoulder. I whirled around. Greasy-Hair, who'd met us at the entrance, frowned. "Pliss to go back to table and eat fast. No loitering and no wandering! This not park, funny bwoay."

Our food had already been served. Now I understood how Greasy-Hair could promise customers a table in thirteen and a half minutes. It was order, eat fast, and get out.

My dish turned out to be an *awesome* choice. The plain *dosa*, a large, crisp wafer made of rice batter, was accompanied by green chutney, coconut chutney, and a sweet-and-sour tomato dipping sauce. It was so incredibly good. I tried not to inhale the food, forcing myself to chew before swallowing.

I tried a bite of Rohit's *idli*, which was a steamed rice cake. It was awesome, too! Mrs. Lal's *thali* was a rainbow array of foods served on a silver platter. In the center was a mound of steaming white rice surrounded by gleaming silver bowls filled with vegetables and lentils. I couldn't identify most of them, but the aromas of ginger, garlic, and fresh cilantro made my mouth water. I wanted to dip a bit of my golden wafer in each of those bowls but held back. Rohit was fine with me tasting his food but I felt shy doing the same with his mom.

"That wasn't too bad," said Rohit with a deep sigh after he'd polished off his third plate of *idlis*.

"You're crazy . . . this was amazing," I said. I'd scarfed down another plain *dosa and* a portion of *idli* with sam-ba and was pleasantly full. "Sure beats mac 'n' cheese and hot dogs."

Mrs. Lal excused herself from the table.

"You could have trusted me, you know," Rohit said the minute Mrs. Lal was out of earshot. Obviously what I'd said earlier was bothering him, like I knew it would. "You didn't have to check with Ma when I recommended a dish."

"Bro, trust has to be earned and on this trip your bank balance is a big fat zero," I said. "I know you're angry about Boa but don't take it out on me! I'm only trying to help."

"Interesting . . ." a gruff voice said. "*Very* interesting."

Together we turned to look at the speaker. A white-haired geezer in a dirty white kurta-pajama sat at the next table toying with a steel glass filled with a brown liquid that was either coffee or masala chai.

"Excuse me?" said Rohit. "What's so interesting?"

The old man stared at us without saying a word. His large, bulbous nose looked like it had been stuck on his heavily lined face as an afterthought. Blossoming on his left cheekbone was a bruise in every shade of purple. He'd definitely been on the wrong side of a fist.

My gut clenched as our eyes met. He looked like a cross between the evil wizard Saruman, from *LOTR*, and Hannibal Lecter, the deranged psychiatrist and serial killer from *The Silence of the Lambs*. I'd snuck *Silence of the Lambs* from my parents' DVD collection on a lonely night, despite being grounded once for watching an R-rated movie. I had nightmares for a week. Not the smartest thing I've done. I turned away, my heart pounding, my hands clammy.

"You two," he said, his black eyes still scrutinizing us.

"Whacko," whispered Rohit under his breath. "Ignore him."

"You bet," I said, turning away from that laser-beam gaze. "Hate to run into him on a dark night."

"Don't say a word to Ma about this geezer trying to talk to us or she'll freak," said Rohit. "She won't let us out of her sight."

"Got it," I said and slurped the last of my mango *lassi*. Even though I liked Mrs. L, I couldn't imagine spending every minute of my trip under her scrutiny. I'd go nuts.

Rohit fiddled with his cell phone while I scrolled through the pictures I'd taken, as we waited for Mrs. Lal to return. A hand landed on my shoulder and I almost dropped my camera. That old man had a lot of nerve. First he freaked us out with his psycho talk and now he was *touching* me. I'd had enough of aggressive beggars, scootie drivers, and other complete strangers manhandling me. I'd show him!

I put the camera on the table. With a bloodcurdling yell (all Bollywood movie actors did this before being heroic) I shot to my feet, grabbed and wrenched his arm off my shoulder, and tackled the geezer to the ground.

Our kid waiter stared up at me from the floor, eyes wide with shock and horror. "Your bill, sir," he said and burst into tears.

A shocked silence fell over the restaurant. None of the patrons were smiling now. Greasy-Hair was livid that a foreigner had attacked his waiter. Mrs. Lal had to do a lot of explaining and give them a hefty tip so they wouldn't report me to the police. I'd apologized profusely to our waiter but he wouldn't even look at me. He zipped straight into the kitchen and didn't show his face again till we left.

Just as we stepped out the door, Greasy-Hair called out, "You are *banned* from this restaurant, madam, bwoays. Do not come back to Sagar or I will call pohleece."

Rohit was chuckling, muttering under his breath. "Let's see . . . cows, kids, and now Sagar. I wonder what else you'll be banned from before this trip is over."

Both Rohit and I were yawning our heads off, so Mrs. Lal suggested heading back to the flat for a short rest before exploring Deolali. Neither of us put up a fight.

· · · · · ·

A few hours later, refreshed and fortified with snacks Mrs. Lal had packed, we set off to check out the main street.

Rohit wasn't too keen, but I agreed. After Mrs. Lal saved me from jail time earlier that day, I wasn't going to disagree with her about anything.

The sidewalks thronged with pedestrians as goats ran between them, dropping dainty pellets of crap. Jaywalkers dodged the slow-moving traffic as they crossed the street. Loud music blared from speakers set up on the sidewalks as each shopkeeper tried to drown out his neighbor. Stray dogs slept wherever they could find room. I shot dozens of pictures, experimenting with different angles and trying to frame the subjects creatively.

"Can we go back now?" asked Rohit after a few minutes. "I'm beat and I want to chill."

"Let's go till the end of the road," I said, still clicking away. "Come on, Ro, stop being a party pooper. I need some exercise and so do you."

"You don't have to agree with everything Ma says, you know," Rohit snapped. "And if you want the truth, I think you have a long way to go before you can win this competition."

I gave him a dirty look. "So you mean I'm not good?"

"I mean, you're not too bad," he said and looked away.

Was he lying just to hurt me because I'd sided with his mom again? What if I really wasn't good and Dad had been right all along?

"Don't say that, Rohit," Mrs. Lal piped in. "I've seen some of Dylan's pictures and they are superb. You do what you have to, *Beta*. Don't let anyone interfere with what your heart says."

"Thanks, Mrs. L."

Saturday morning at Chez Moore. Dad had just gotten back from playing tennis with a friend and was lounging by the pool reading the Wall Street Journal. *Even at his age he was in real good shape.*

"Dad?"

His blue eyes locked with mine. "Yeah, son?"

"Could you order the soft-filter lens for me before I leave for India? I'll pay you back from my allowance."

Dad's face tightened and he looked away. Silence except for the pool filter whispering softly.

"This is all such a waste of time and money," Dad finally said.

The sunlight seemed to dim. The green of the trees faded. Even the pool filter hiccupped and fell silent. "I don't agree, Dad."

He stared at me for a long moment. I met his gaze, forcing myself not to look away first.

"All right, Dylan," he said at last. His words were soft and low, tinged with deep disappointment. "Send me the specifications and I'll order it. But this is the last one. If I'm going to pour money into this hobby, I'd like to see concrete results."

"And if I win a competition, no matter which place, you'll get off my case?"

"Yes."

"We have a deal," I said, feeling elated and depressed all at once. I wanted to be a photographer, but not with this kind of pressure. But I'd have to do it, and win, to shut him up once and for all.

Rohit's words cut deeper than Dad's. But I was going to prove them both wrong. When I held the camera, Dylan the clumsy guy melted away and someone else took over. I really liked being a photographer; it made me feel good about myself.

The air was still and thick, as if a thundershower was imminent. Rohit marched ahead, his back straight. I followed, determined to talk to him at the flat. I was getting tired of our constant arguing and his mean jabs.

I also wanted to explain *why* winning was so important to me but a thought nagged at me. Why did I have to explain anything at all? Why couldn't he just be my friend and go with what made me happy, like I did with him? Resentment bubbled up and made me feel twisted up inside. I tried to focus on my surroundings as I snapped a picture of a kid nestled against a sleeping goat. Definitely an unusual friendship. I looked at the shot I'd taken, my heart beating hard. It looked good but the reflection of traffic in the window behind them marred the picture. I couldn't use this one. By the time I raised my camera for another shot, the goat had woken up and wandered away.

It was dark by the time we got to the end of the main street. Only a few lights illuminated the deserted road beyond. There must have been houses past the lights but it felt like we were near Mordor.

"A bustling main street behind me, and up ahead, nothing," I said. "It's like we're at the edge of a vast wasteland teeming with wildlife."

Mrs. Lal laughed. "Good imagination, Dylan, but there's no *wildlife* here except rabbits, squirrels, an occasional fox, and plenty of snakes. Since this is a military base for the Artillery Division of the Indian Army, building permits are rarely given. The residential area starts beyond this point and is, unfortunately, not very well lit. This small town goes to sleep by ten in the evening at the very latest. It wouldn't be fun getting lost, so promise me you won't venture there after dark?"

"You got it, Mrs. L."

"Can we go now?" asked Rohit, sounding utterly bored. "There's no chance I'll be wandering around after dark. I'd rather read a book."

"Just a little farther, boys," said Mrs. Lal. "There's something I want you both to see."

Rohit huffed and strode on ahead while I followed at a leisurely pace with Mrs. Lal. We walked for another couple of minutes, leaving the main street behind. Around us the darkness gathered, a light or two twinkling through the tree-lined streets.

"Where are we going, Ma?" asked Rohit. He'd stopped in the middle of the sidewalk. "I've had enough. I'm going back."

The air was thick and heavy. Mosquitoes buzzed around my eyes and ears. I slapped a couple of them and felt something wet against my cheek. Gross.

"Look up," said Mrs. Lal.

We looked up at a black canopy, every inch studded with stars. A pizza-crust sliver of moon hung between bright jewels. I wished I had a lens powerful enough to capture it. I focused on enjoying the view instead.

"Awesome," I breathed. "Back home you'd have to go pretty far outside the city to see a sky like this."

"I know," she said softly. "That's why I thought you'd like to see it."

For once even Rohit was silent.

"A shooting star!" said Mrs. Lal. "Quick, make a wish."

I wished I still had a family when I got back home and concentrated on the star till it disappeared.

As we walked back to the flat, I wondered what Rohit had wished for. First, he'd probably wish to go home to New York. Or maybe he'd wish for everything I had: lots of money, a big house, and a pool. All the stuff that made life comfortable and you could grow to love. But could never love you back.

TWELVE

B Y THE TIME WE GOT BACK I WAS DRIPPING WITH sweat, as if I'd had a shower with all my clothes on. I needed to rinse off before bed, but Rohit cut me off as I reached the bathroom.

"Hey, I was here first!" I said, wiping my face on the sleeve of my T-shirt.

"Why? So you could check to see if the toilet was returned?" he said and slammed the door in my face.

It was such a sad joke, I couldn't even muster a smile. I was seething but, with Mrs. Lal there, I couldn't knock any (literal) sense into him.

Note to Self: If Rohit wants to see mean, it's time to show him mean!

Mrs. Lal shook her head. "Sorry, Dylan, I don't know what's gotten into him. Maybe Anjali is right. This whole immigration thing was a very bad idea. He might be better off in India."

I stared at her, my heart racing. Rohit was playing right into Boa's coils with his moodiness. If he didn't stop *now*, he was staying.

"He'll be fine once we get back to New York," I said, watching her face. "*You* know that, don't you?"

She shook her head. "I don't know anything at the moment, but I'll talk to Rohit's father before making a decision."

"He's the best friend I have and I don't want to lose him," I said. Though, right this minute, I could have cheerfully strangled him.

"Goodnight, Dylan," said Mrs. Lal. She walked into her bedroom and shut the door softly.

$$\bullet \ \bullet \ \bullet \ \bullet \ \bullet$$

Rohit was already asleep (or pretending to be) when I got to our room after my shower. I turned on my laptop, hoping I'd be lucky enough to piggyback on someone else's Wi-Fi so I could check if there was a message from Mom.

I did, there was, and it sucked. Mom and Dad had finally agreed on a trial separation but they still loved me *a lot*. Mom would move to an apartment just before school started in September, and Dad would stay in our brownstone. I could choose who I wanted to live with. I read the words again and again, hoping I might have made a mistake the first time. They hadn't changed and neither would the situation waiting for me in New York.

I snapped the laptop shut, resisting the urge to fling it across the room. As if telling me they loved me could make up for the fact that from this point on we were three people, not one family. I lay on the hot mattress staring at a fat lizard chasing mosquitoes. Nothing had worked, not the *hijda*'s blessing or the wish on the shooting star. I was doomed.

All I had left now was Rohit and I was willing to do anything to make sure he came back with me.

· · · · · ·

The most unexpected sound woke me the next morning. I sat up, confused. The fan whirred noisily and I knew it wasn't what had jolted me awake. Then I heard it again: *cock-a-doodle-doo*. I'd only *read* about a rooster's crow and here was a real live one! I jumped out of bed and ran to the window. The sun was just coming up and there sat a red rooster on the roof of the adjacent building, its chest puffed out, trying in earnest to wake the world.

A cool breeze fanned my face. I hurried out of the tiny bedroom and made a beeline for the balcony. The door was already open and an incredible sunrise greeted me. My heart felt lighter in spite of the email from Mom that had weighed on my chest like a fat cat till I'd fallen asleep. Mesmerized, I watched the fiery ball turn everything it touched to gold, climbing higher into the pale-pink sky. This was the second sunrise I'd seen in two days. Mornings in New York were made to rush-order. There was no time to stand still or gaze out the window. At the summer camps I'd been to, I'd dawdled so much the counselors had given up on trying to get me out of the cabin early enough to see the sunrise.

"Beautiful, isn't it?" someone said softly.

Startled, I whirled around. Mrs. Lal stepped onto the balcony holding out a steaming mug of hot chocolate. She'd brought tea for herself.

"Thank you, Mrs. L," I said and took the mug from her. I wrapped my hands around it, feeling the warmth seep through my chilly fingers. It had been scorching when I'd hit the bed last night but toward morning it had cooled down and I'd finally managed to fall asleep.

We sipped from our mugs in silence. Sunlight turned the dewdrops on the foliage around us into liquid gold. I wanted to rush in and get my camera, but didn't want to miss a moment of this perfect morning. Maybe tomorrow I could take some pictures. "This place is so peaceful," I said. "It's like being in another world."

"Yes," Mrs. Lal said. "You have to learn to stand still to really appreciate it. Back in New York one never gets the time. That is why I like coming here whenever possible. In Deolali you can slow down and savor life, if only for a few days. Mr. Lal loves it here, too. It gives him a chance to recharge."

Mom and Dad were always rushing around like crazy. Even at a party, they were busy circulating, making contacts, and working the room from end to end. And now they had rushed right out of each other's lives. Before I could reply, the silence was rudely shattered.

"Hey, Dylan, Ma . . . Where are you guys?"

"You gotta see this, Ro," I called. "Come to the balcony."

Rohit stepped out a few moments later, yawning loudly.

"Morning."

"Good morning, *Beta*. Sleep well?" Mrs. Lal asked.

"Stupid mosquitoes kept me up half the night," he grumbled.

"Didn't you put on that Odomos cream your mom gave us?" I said.

Rohit glared at me, scratching at the tiny red welts covering his bare arms. It was obvious he hadn't. The cream smelled disgusting. I'd gotten used to it after a few minutes but the mosquitoes hadn't. I didn't have a single bite on me.

"I'll get breakfast started," Mrs. Lal said and went back inside.

"Why did you call me here?" Rohit asked as he rubbed his arms and looked around.

"There in front of you," I said, waving at the gold-flecked sky and green fields.

He stared at it for a moment. "S'okay," he said. "Hey, you're the photographer, not me, so don't expect me to gush."

"Listen," I said, my voice dropping to a whisper. "I talked to your mom yesterday."

"And?" Rohit said, suddenly alert.

"She's going to discuss this whole mess with your dad when he gets here. But till then you gotta stay cool, Ro. I mean it. You're playing right into Boa's hands by acting like a jerk."

Rohit frowned. "If we'd stayed in New York, none of this would be happening. I wish I hadn't let you convince me to go on this trip."

"If only you hadn't barfed on Boa and screwed up the plan we talked about, your mom wouldn't even *consider* the insane option of leaving you here."

Rohit glared at me. "Stop lecturing me! I already have Ma for that."

Sunlight bathed his scrunched-up face. I took a deep breath. We were having a fight every waking minute and it was really lame. I needed his support just as much as he needed mine, even though he didn't know it yet.

"We're going exploring today, and we're going to talk. Okay?"

"Yeah, we'll talk," he said, staring into the distance. "Though I don't know how that's going to help."

As I watched him I thought of the video I'd taken of Boa threatening Mrs. L at the reception. It was my trump card but I'd let them work things out on their own before I interfered. And given how mean Rohit had been lately, he deserved to stew a bit.

• • • • • •

"Breakfast is ready," Mrs. Lal called out. "Wash up and come to the dining table."

Rohit and I raced to brush our teeth. I stared at my reflection in the mirror. My short blond hair, blue eyes, and athletic build were a stark contrast to Rohit's tall, thin frame, curly black hair, and black eyes. I'd been teased a lot about how weird we looked together, but that had never mattered to me.

142

Now I was beginning to wonder if what was on the inside was more different than I realized.

Breakfast was toast, butter, and strawberry jam with a choice of hot chocolate or tea. Mrs. Lal had laid it all out on the dining table. From where we sat, we could look out the open balcony door. I buttered a slice of toast and munched it, gazing at the lush green treetops swaying in the breeze. The *dosas* and *idlis* from yesterday were a distant memory and I was ravenous.

"Can't we have bacon and eggs?" asked Rohit.

"You know I didn't have time to shop yesterday," said Mrs. Lal, an edge to her voice. "This is what I carried from Mumbai. If you don't like it, don't eat it."

Careful, Ro, I wanted to warn him. I sipped my hot chocolate instead, knowing it wouldn't help if I spoke up.

Rohit took a slice of toast, spread it liberally with jam, and nibbled on it. There were still some cold vibes between them and I was caught in the middle. I had no clue how this would turn out except that his moodiness was getting on my nerves, ruining our vacation, and affecting our friendship. It was also the last thing either of us needed right now.

The sun climbed higher in the sky and so did the temperature. The cool tile floor was already warming up under my bare feet. Today was going to be another scorcher.

"What are you boys planning this morning?"

"I'd like to go biking," I said. "Rohit can show me around. Yeah?"

"Good idea," said Mrs. Lal. "I'll get some groceries and meet you back at the flat for lunch. Rohit, we have to meet your father at the station at three. Make sure you're back by noon."

"Do I have to go biking?" he said, not meeting my eye. "I'd rather stay here and read."

"Dylan is your guest and you will show him around," Mrs. Lal said. "I want no further discussion on this."

"Yes, Ma!" he said through gritted teeth.

"Come on, Ro," I said when we were alone. "Lolly-land can't be that bad."

"Wait till you see the rest of this place. In some ways it's worse than Mumbai."

His expression was one of anger mixed with resignation. I promised myself: Today we were going to have that *talk*. I was going to knock some sense into my friend or knock him senseless, depending on how things went.

THIRTEEN

WE GOT DRESSED AT WARP SPEED FOR A QUICK getaway, but still couldn't escape the head-splitting barrage of instructions from Rohit's mom. My ears were ringing as we fled downstairs. Mom rarely bothered to give me instructions when I was leaving except to remind me to call if I was going to be late, and to text our driver as soon as I was ready to be picked up. I really missed Mom's laid-back style, especially with Mrs. Lal in overdrive, treating us like little kids.

"Stay together and don't go too far. Remember, don't talk to strangers."

Rohit and I had bolted out the door while she was still talking. As soon as we emerged from the building, she continued from the balcony.

"Are you carrying your cell phone, Rohit?"

"Yes, Ma!"

"The cell phone coverage is very bad around here, so try and check in whenever you can, especially if you see a missed call from me. Do you remember our address?"

"Ma, it's all in my phone. We're twelve and you're treating us like babies," he said, rolling his eyes.

"Yes, *Beta*," Mrs. Lal said, "but many roads have been renamed since we last came here and this is the first time you're going off exploring without your father or me. The landmarks you used to know are gone. Just . . . be careful. Come back by noon!"

"*Okaaay*, Ma!" "Yes, Mrs. Lal!" we said in unison and galloped down the street, out of earshot.

"Shall we hold hands?" I said, sidling up to him.

Rohit immediately swerved away from me. "Are you nuts? People will laugh at us."

"Well, your mom did ask us to *stay together*," I said, trying to keep a straight face. "Come on, you can't disobey her."

"You touch me and I'll punch you," he huffed. "What's wrong with you?" A drop of sweat slid down his temple and dangled at his jaw. He swiped at it and continued walking.

"You punch me and I'll sit on you. You'll be flatter than a *chapati*!"

We stared at each other for a second and burst out laughing. It wasn't like old times but it was a start.

"There's a bike shop just down this street," said Rohit. "We can rent bikes there."

"Sounds like a plan," I said, dabbing my forehead with my sleeve. It was only ten in the morning and I was already wilting. I kept reminding myself that the heat and exercise would help me become a lean, mean machine. I shouldn't complain too much.

A three-wheeler roared past and on its side was that same weird lady with the six arms we'd seen on Khan's scootie. The snack was there, too—lemons and chilies hanging on a thread and powdered with soot. I wouldn't touch it if it was the last bit of food left in India.

"That lady sure is popular with a lot of guys. And what's with the seasonings near the exhaust pipe?"

Rohit laughed. "That's Kali Ma, a Hindu goddess. She's supposed to protect her worshipers from harm. The lemon-chilies combo is to ward off the evil eye."

"Odd," I said, "but I guess whatever floats their boat . . ."

"In India, no one messes with tradition, dude, even if it makes no sense at all."

"If you say so."

We turned the corner and there was the shop with gleaming bicycles lined up on the sidewalk in a neat row, padlocked to a post by a rusty chain woven through them. MANU'S CYCLE SHOP the sign above the store declared.

"Here we are," said Rohit.

"Hello, *darlings*," the owner said, sauntering toward us. Manu was a short guy in tight white jeans, a white shirt, and a pink handkerchief that was tied around his neck. Somehow he smelled of *jalebis* and I felt hungry even though we'd just eaten breakfast.

"We'll take two bikes," said Rohit. "Till noon."

Manu unlocked the chain and wheeled out two shiny bikes. "That'll be two hundred rupees for the morning." Red juice trickled down the side of his mouth, which was constantly moving like a cow chewing its cud. He wiped the mess away with a grubby handkerchief.

"No way," said Rohit, staring at Manu from the top of his glasses. "I'll pay you a hundred or we're going to—"

"Tanu's Bikes," I piped in, pointing to a rival's shop across the street.

Manu glared at me. Another trickle of red liquid oozed from the corner of his mouth. Up came the grubby hankie. It was gross and I looked away.

"Okay, *darlings*," said Manu. "For you, *special* price. You pay me hundred and fifty rupees."

After a bit more haggling, Rohit gave him a hundred and twenty-five rupees. Manu winked and pocketed it.

"How much is that in USD?" I asked as we wheeled the bikes along the sidewalk.

"About two bucks," said Rohit. He adjusted the height of the seat and went over his bike more thoroughly than Harry Potter examining the Marauder's Map for Snape's whereabouts.

"Wow! If my family lived here, we'd be gazillionaires."

"You already are," said Rohit as he started to pedal away. "No need to rub my nose in it."

I jumped onto my bike and caught up with him. "Can you stop that?" I yelled over the din of traffic.

"Stop what?" asked Rohit, not looking at me.

"This flip-flopping," I said. "One minute you're laughing and the next, you're punking me and biting my head off.

Jekyll and Hyde were more consistent. You have a pretty decent life here in India and a great family. Do you know how lucky you are?"

"I'm lucky?" said Rohit. "What about *you*? You're a trust-fund baby. You'll never have to worry about money! If we had a hundredth of what you have, we wouldn't be at Bua's mercy all the time."

"Oh, shut up!" I snapped. "You're not the only one with problems. Once in a while, take your head out of the sand and look around. You might be surprised to see that the world doesn't revolve around you."

"What d'you mean?" he said. "If you have a problem, spit it out."

"I don't want to talk about it right now."

"Then why bring it up?" he said, giving me an odd look. "You've been acting weird since we got to Mumbai."

"Me?" I shot back. "You could win the world championship for whacko!"

We continued in silence. I was seriously pissed. I thought I knew Rohit but I'd really known only one *avatar* of his—the sensitive and loyal one back home, desperately trying to fit in, just like I was.

It was an unspoken rule that every newb had to obey the class bullies for a day. If they asked him to climb a tree, he did it. If they asked him to run across the street in traffic, he had to do that, too. Those who didn't listen were picked on for the rest of the year. I overheard which day the bullies had picked for Rohit and I warned him to stay home sick.

When I saw him in class the next day I was mad at him and grudgingly proud. This guy had guts, which I mostly lacked. Rohit did get picked on to do the most ridiculous things, and when he refused, they ganged up on him after school. I felt like I had to jump in and help out. In the end we all got detention for fighting.

I expected the bullying to continue but they'd worked out another plan to make us squirm. Everyone in class had been warned to ignore Ro and me, or else. I was used to being a loner but at least once in a while I'd get a smile or a "Hey there." I was pretty much invisible at home and now it was like I didn't exist at school, either. It felt worse than being beaten up.

Lunchtime was torture. No matter where I sat, my classmates would get up, leaving me to eat by myself.

Rohit normally avoided the cafeteria by bringing a packed lunch and finding a little nook to eat and read in.

A couple of days after the boycotting, he turned up and started sitting with me. That was when I knew we had each other's backs.

Our fellowship had worked out really well. Till now. Just like the One Ring had changed Frodo, Mumbai and Boa were changing Ro into a stranger. I had to stop it somehow.

"We have to go back," I said suddenly. "We forgot the rest of the gear."

"What gear?" said Rohit, continuing to pedal and dodge pedestrians.

"Helmet, shin pads, wrist guards, you know . . . all the safety stuff."

Rohit looked back briefly, frowning. "Look around, Dylan. See anyone here wearing that stuff?"

He was right. People zipped past in both directions carrying ungainly merchandise—stuff that should have been in a pickup truck or a van was artfully secured on their bikes. There were large aluminum milk cans, dozens of bags filled with empty bottles, even an entire family. But there wasn't a single helmet in sight, and definitely no wrist guards.

"Dylan, even if you had a helmet, I wouldn't let you wear it," said Rohit. "You already stand out like a sore thumb. Remember that crazy old guy at Sagar? It's better not to draw any more attention to yourself."

"Point taken," I said, thankful he was still watching my back in spite of his miserable mood swings.

We headed out of the congested downtown area toward the residential streets. Cycling was hard, but I welcomed the opportunity to burn a few extra calories. Maybe Dad would notice. Mom, too. I ignored the dull ache in my chest at the thought of them and focused on the road so I wouldn't get run over.

This was so much better than walking and I was starting to

get good at avoiding the numerous obstacles, man and beast. The one road rule that prevailed was simple: The strong had right-of-way and the weak ran for their lives.

Soon we'd left the traffic behind and were cycling along a tree-lined street dappled with sunshine. The gas fumes and food smells were thinning and I could suck in a lungful of relatively clean air.

"Where are we going?" I asked, enjoying the cool breeze on my face. It was a relief not to have to dodge oncoming traffic as we cycled along at a good speed.

"Canyon Hill. It's a steep ride to the top but the view isn't bad," said Rohit. "I used to like going there as a kid. You can photograph the abandoned canyon from up there."

"Any chance of stopping for a breather?" I asked, pumping away, the camera swinging like a heavy pendulum from my neck.

The road snaked between banyan trees, their long, brown roots hanging from the branches. I was already tempted to get off and take a short break under their cool canopies but I also wanted to get to the top of the hill for an aerial shot of Lolly-land.

"Keep going. We'll stop at a farm along the way," said Rohit. "We can buy freshly picked grapes—good on a scorcher like today."

"Cool!"

Whitewashed houses flashed by between trees bearing bright-red flowers. They looked like drops of blood on the green leaves, their sweet smell perfuming the air. Gulmohar, Rohit informed me when I insisted we stop so I could take a couple of pictures. They looked fantastic against the blue sky.

A cow ambled across the road just as we continued on our way. I rang the bell but she didn't look up. I stopped.

"Don't you *dare*!" said Rohit. "Even if you think no one's watching, someone is. And this time we don't have Ma to save us."

"I wasn't going to," I said. *"Honest."* Not true. I'd been planning to charge it, just to see how fast it would run to get out of the way.

"Yeah, right," said Rohit with a snort. "I know you, Dylan Moore."

"You're wrong," I replied, though we both knew he wasn't.

We turned off the main road after about half an hour. I was panting and melting, in no particular order. I expected to turn into a puddle at any second. A long and dusty road undulated before us, green fields on either side dotted with houses and barns. Not a soul in sight.

"Burning up, bro. Gotta take a break," I gasped, then hopped off the bike and wheeled it to a shady spot under a tree.

"You look like a cooked lobster, Dylan," Rohit said. "You okay? You're not planning on dying on me, are you?" He pushed his glasses up and stared at me.

"Water," I gasped.

"How about cold lemonade?" he asked.

I nodded. My tongue seemed swollen and my throat was parched and scratchy. Mrs. Lal had insisted Rohit carry a thermos in his backpack and now I was glad. I accepted a cupful and chugged it. Rohit gulped a cupful, too.

"Better?" he said.

"Please, sir, I want some more."

Rohit chuckled, and poured me half a cup. He screwed the lid back on. "That's all you're getting for now. We better ration it because we're going to need it when we get to the top." He reached out a hand to pull me up and just for a moment I glimpsed my old friend: nerdy and serious, but with a ready smile and a generous heart. "Let's go," he said. "Or we'll never make it back in time and Ma's going to have a cow."

"A mother having a mother," I said. "Interesting."

Rohit punched me in the arm. I punched him back and immediately grabbed him before he toppled over. All was well. For now.

We got onto our bikes and started pedaling. A bunch of cute girls in shorts and T-shirts cycled past us. I smiled at them and they smiled back.

"Where are those girls coming from? This place looks deserted," I said, trying to balance and look behind me.

"Barnes," said Rohit.

I almost cycled into a ditch. "You mean those girls were raised in a barn? Let's go check it out. Has to be *way* cooler than a grape farm!"

Rohit laughed so hard his bike wobbled precariously. "*Barnes*, with an *e*, is the local co-ed boarding school. I almost went there but Ma decided I was better off in a private school in Mumbai."

"Let's go back and invite them for a cool lassi . . . and samosa. I guess."

"This place isn't so backward. There's Coke and pizza here, too," said Rohit. The edge was back in his voice. "And no, we're not going back. You wanted to see the sights, not meet girls."

"*Joking*, Ro. Lighten up." He'd become ultrasensitive, always taking my comments as a slight on his previous home even when they weren't. Come on! This was my best bud and I shouldn't have to choose my words carefully every time I spoke to him.

"Whatever," he said, picking up speed.

"Wait! We have to go back. We've lost something really important!"

"What?" Rohit slowed and looked back over his shoulder.

"Your sense of humor."

"Ha-ha," he said and sped away.

And just like that my best friend from a few minutes ago vanished and a grumpy doppelganger took his place. I almost wished we were back in New York. There, I could text my driver to pick me up and go home. Out here we were stuck together whether we liked it or not. And right now I didn't.

The road sloped uphill and Rohit took the lead. I caught up to him and then we were pumping hard, each wanting to reach the top first. My lungs were on fire and the rest of me ached like I had the flu. It felt like someone had tied chains to my legs and was pulling me down. Rohit panted hard, his glasses ready to dive off his nose. He didn't stop even to push them up.

When we finally reached the top of Canyon Hill, neck and neck, my heart was ready to burst out of my chest. My pulse drumming in my ear, I looked back at the steep incline. I was amazed I'd made it this far without dying. And it felt good! I surveyed the landscape as intently as the cool Legolas in *The Fellowship of the Ring*, when they'd been in hot pursuit of the Orcs to rescue the hobbits. I'd seen the movie so often, I could hear the soundtrack during this particular scene in my mind.

"This is awesome," I wheezed.

"Yup," said Rohit, lying flat on his back, breathing hard.

I wanted to lie down and rest, too, but the light was just right and I didn't want to waste a good photo op. I started clicking.

"Can you stop with the manic photography session for a few minutes?" asked Rohit, sitting up. He unpacked his backpack and took out slices of chocolate cake and the lemonade. "Other than that canyon there are no pictures for your friendship theme up here."

"Nope," I said, focusing the lens on a bee resting inside a bright-yellow flower. Not really what I was looking for but it was too good a picture to pass up. "You're the one who suggested iStock for extra cash. These pictures are for my portfolio so shut up and let me focus."

"Why do I get the feeling this isn't only about the competition? You're hiding something from me, dude."

"And I told you, Dad thinks I'm wasting his money on this silly yet expensive hobby. He wants to see results on every dime he spends. So, I have to win something."

Rohit flicked his glasses up. "He has a point."

"What?" I said, lowering the camera. "You agree that any activity should be pursued only if there's something to gain? You're as nuts as he is."

"Look what happens when you're not rich or when you're financially dependent on someone," he said bitterly. "They think they can dictate your life."

"Like Boa," I said.

"Like Boa," he echoed, staring into the distance. "If Dad succumbs to her bullying like he normally does, my life's over. She's a human bulldozer when it comes to handling objections. I hate her!"

I sat down next to him and helped myself to cake. "So we fight it using strategy, not tantrums. Don't forget—your mom's tough and she loves you even if you've been acting like an idiot lately. Any suggestions?"

Rohit gave me a dirty look. "Tell Ma and Papa you want to go home, *ASAP*. And tell them you refuse to travel alone. We all have to go with you."

"That's seriously stupid, bro!" I said. "I'm not doing it."

"After all I've done for you, you can't tell a little lie for me?" he snapped. "Some *best* friend!"

"*Shut up!* Even if I insist I want to go home tonight, do you really think she'll drop everything and go? After all the money you guys have spent on the tickets, do you think she'd want to waste—" I stopped, seeing Rohit's murderous expression.

"Go on," he taunted. "Finish what you were saying. You meant when we're so poor."

"You're *not* poor!" I said. "You have everything you need to make you happy."

My wealth had never bothered him back home and now suddenly he kept throwing it in my face. "And stop using my money as an excuse to behave like a spaz. Maybe if you stopped whining so much, your mom wouldn't consider leaving you behind, which I know for a fact she's thinking about right now." I knew I'd gone too far but I was really mad at him.

Rohit stood there twitching like a puppet on a sugar high. "You're pathetic, Dylan. I wish I'd *never* invited you here."

"Ha! And you think *you're* a good friend? All the mean tricks you've been playing since we got to Mumbai? The mood swings? They're seriously lame and so are you. I came here to have a good time, to escape my parents who're always complaining about how I should do better. I know I'm not perfect but at least I'm not a whiny baby like you."

"You're nothing but a rich, spoiled doofus," he said in a tight, low voice. *"Rich. Spoiled. Doofus."* He spoke slowly, enunciating each word as if I'd missed it the first time.

It felt as if I were having a heart attack. I remembered all the mean things bullies had shouted at me over the years. But I'd never expected to hear them from my best friend. My Frodo. A zinger teetered at the tip of my tongue. I stopped. Would we stop being friends if I said it aloud? But what kind of a person would I be if I couldn't be honest when I had to?

I took a deep breath. "I'm not ashamed of being rich. But I hate when you keep reminding me about it. You know what *your* problem is? You're shallow. If you had any brains, you'd realize you're really lucky and stop envying me. *Mean. Shallow. Wimp.* That's what *you* are." Even as I spat out the words, I knew I'd said too much. But now that they were out, there was no taking them back. By either of us.

"Thank you for reminding me of my shortcomings," he said coldly. "I tend to forget when I'm with a friend." His face was white and for once he was absolutely still, which was even scarier than all the twitching. "Let's head back."

"I'm sorry, Ro," I blurted out, instantly ashamed I'd lost my temper and hurt him, even though he'd done the same to me. After all, I was a guest in his home and his country, and I had to be the bigger person. "You know I didn't mean it like that . . . it just slipped out. You're my best bud. I love you like the brother I never had. Haven't I always watched your back?"

"Right," sneered Rohit. "You're just like all the other snobs at school. I should have known I was just an assignment to you. You're too self-centered to be a real friend and you have the nerve to blame it on me. You know what? If you were the last person on earth, I wouldn't want you as a friend."

It's as if the Ringwraith at the watchtower of Amon Sûl pierced me *instead of Frodo with a Morgul-blade.* "I know the curveball Boa threw wasn't what we'd expected on vacation but we could have solved this together. We still can if you stop being so pigheaded."

"Just forget it!" said Rohit, his voice shaking. "You're too selfish to think of anything but getting pictures and entering that dumb photography contest. The rest of the time you stuff your face and suck up to my family. What kind of a friend does that?" He turned away, his spine ramrod straight, his fists clenched at his sides.

I was so tempted to push him off the hill. "I was doing it to be polite, not to show you up. And there's nothing wrong with appreciating good food. You think you have it bad? Try living *my* life for a change. Then we'll compare notes."

"I would love to!" he said, glaring at me. "Must be so *hard* to live in such luxury, a million servants at your beck and call, and never having to worry about money."

My spacious house flashed through my mind. It had six bedrooms, seven bathrooms, a gym, game room, pool, terrace, and home theater. And of course there was the cooking-show-quality kitchen filled with the latest and most expensive appliances. But it was cold and mostly empty. Often, Rohit had asked me if he could come over. I'd agreed a couple of times when Mom and Dad were away on business trips and only the housekeeper, gardener, and driver were around. Most of the time I went to his tiny apartment, where his room—though smaller than our broom closet—felt more like home than mine ever did. This guy was richer than I was and he was too dumb to know it. But he wouldn't listen to me now and I wasn't going to show him how much his words had hurt me. Somehow I burst out laughing, though I really wanted to cry.

Something snapped inside Rohit. He shoved me so hard I sat down on the grass, winded. For a minute I could only look at him in utter shock. Rohit, who'd rescue an ant from the sidewalk so it wouldn't get stepped on, had pushed me. I jumped to my feet and shoved him back. And this time I didn't bother to grab him. His glasses flew off his nose as he fell backward, landing on his bony butt with a thump.

"That hurt!" he said, his voice trembling. "You're such a loser."

"Ditto, *bud*," I said, trying to swallow the lump in my throat. Our long-awaited talk had spiraled totally out of control and there was nothing I could do to stop or reverse it. "You're right about one thing—this trip was a mistake. I can't wait to get home."

Just the thought of home made me sick. But *this* made me want to barf. I'd had arguments with Rohit before but none had been this bad.

Rohit was on all fours groping around for his glasses. I knew he was blind as a bat without them. For a moment I watched him but he stubbornly refused to ask for help. Finally I couldn't stand it anymore. I picked up his glasses and jammed them onto his nose. He adjusted them and stood up without a word.

"Shall we head back?" he said in an excruciatingly polite voice, as if he were talking to a stranger.

"Yes, please," I replied, equally polite.

We mounted our bikes and coasted downhill. When I glanced back at the horizon, dark rain clouds had gathered, blotting out the sun.

FOURTEEN

A S SOON AS WE WALKED THROUGH THE DOOR, Mrs. Lal's face lit up like the Christmas tree in Rockefeller Center. A twinge of jealousy stirred in my heart. I couldn't remember the last time Mom or Dad had been around when I'd walked through the door, let alone looked excited to see me.

"Had a good time, boys?" she asked, switching off the radio, silencing what sounded exactly like Minnie Mouse being tortured.

"Yes, Mrs. L," I said, trying to muster a smile. "It was great."

"Yes, Ma," Rohit answered. "What's for lunch?"

"Chicken biryani," she said. "Your favorite, Rohit. And I know you love it, too, Dylan."

So *that* was the fantastic scent perfuming the air. After all that exercise I knew I could eat to my heart's content.

"Go wash up. We'll eat, rest for a bit, and then head to the station," she said. "Why the long faces? Is everything okay?"

I knew she'd notice and I just wasn't up to a barrage of questions. "Gotta go to the bathroom," I mumbled and hurried off. This time there wasn't a peep out of Rohit about the stolen toilet. I actually missed his stupid joke.

Mrs. Lal was having a whispered conversation with Rohit that stopped as soon as I stepped out of the bathroom to wash my hands in the sink located outside. I scrubbed away. The silence stretched. When I couldn't delay any longer, I joined them at the table. A pot of chicken cooked in yogurt and spices and mixed with rice sat in the center of the table, steaming gently. There was also some *raita* with fresh mint leaves to cut the spice of the biryani.

"So, where did you go?" asked Mrs. Lal as she ladled out generous portions of the rice and chicken onto our plates and topped them with a dollop of the yogurt *raita*. I couldn't wait to dig in.

"Canyon Hill," I answered and took a huge bite of food so I'd have an excuse to keep my mouth shut.

"It used to be one of Rohit's favorite places," she said. "Did you like going back?"

"It was okay," said Rohit, his eyes glued to his plate, his voice subdued.

"What about you, Dylan?"

What *was* it with all these questions? Too much attention could get pretty annoying and Mrs. Lal's antenna was up twenty-four seven. Rohit and I mumbled answers in turn. I wished she'd just stop with the grilling and let us eat in peace.

Finally Mrs. Lal got the hint and started eating. She mixed the rice and chicken with her fingers and popped a morsel into her mouth. I watched as she ate, with barely a grain of rice falling out between her fingertips. If I knew how, I'd have liked to have tried it, too. But I was too hungry to fiddle around with my food.

Rohit pushed the biryani around on his plate with a fork, occasionally shooting dark looks at his mom as she ate with her fingers. He ignored me completely. I polished off the first helping and took seconds.

"Eat, *Beta*," Mrs. Lal cajoled Rohit. "You're too thin as it is. Finish what's on your plate."

"I'm not hungry, Ma."

"I worked all morning to make your favorite dish, Rohit, but hungry or not, you will finish what's on your plate. There are too many starving children in the world. No one is wasting food in my house."

And that was that. We ate the remainder of the meal in silence. I felt Mrs. Lal's eyes study us from time to time but thankfully she didn't ask any more questions.

The food hit the spot, but I wasn't any happier than when I'd sat down. My friend was still not talking to me and I was afraid it would be a very long time before things went back to normal. If they ever did.

· · · · · ·

The station thronged with people and the din was deafening. Even in the searing afternoon heat, porters ran to and fro carrying luggage and sweating so much, their shirts were glued to their backs. I could barely stumble along in the heat and even the *thought* of carrying a book to read while we waited made me break out in buckets of sweat. My respect for porters and working-class Indians skyrocketed. They lived such a harsh life and yet they soldiered on without complaining. They never gave up or admitted defeat. If I could be *half* as persevering, no one would be able to stop me from following my dream. Not even Dad.

We waited in a small tea shop across from the station. It had precisely five rickety tables with cracked and dirty plastic tops. The blades of the ceiling fan rotated sluggishly, its wire guts spilling out the sides. I expected it to crash down on my head at any minute. The place had a strong smell of fried foods and the shop's special cardamom tea.

Mrs. Lal ordered bottles of Thums Up for Rohit and me, and a tea for herself, explaining that drinking something hot on a scorching day was actually very cooling. I assumed she was suffering from a touch of sunstroke, and nodded politely.

"How do these people have the stamina to work in this heat?" I said, taking a long slurp of my Thums Up.

"They have to make a living and feed their families," said Mrs. Lal. "They can't stay home complaining about the heat or they'll die of starvation. And anyway, they're used to it."

No wonder I'd never heard Rohit complain about the heat in New York. After living through these temperatures, a hundred degrees must be a joke. I never did understand why he'd roll his eyes when the Weather Channel issued a heat alert. Now I knew. I was melting by the pound and seriously contemplating sneaking into the kitchen and climbing into their freezer.

We sat in silence for a couple of minutes while I examined my beat-up glass bottle. I wondered if there was any more news from Mom and made a mental note to log in when we got back to the flat. I didn't want to, but knew I had to. I was desperately hoping they would change their minds. I was surrounded by people but, with no one to confide in, I'd never felt more alone in my life.

"Is there a place I can make a long-distance call from?" I asked Mrs. Lal.

She took a sip of her tea, thinking hard. "Yes, lots of them. Why?"

"I thought I'd say hi to my mom," I said.

"Good idea. We can call right after we pick up Rohit's dad. Would you like that?" Her eyes bored into me and I wondered how much she knew or guessed.

"Thanks . . . maybe tomorrow," I replied. "Just show me the place and I can call on my own." I wanted to hear Mom's voice but I didn't want to make the call with Rohit's family watching. Maybe I'd go tomorrow and make the call while he was sorting out his own problems with his parents. I had more than enough rupees with me.

"Ok, *Beta*, I'll have Uncle show you the phone kiosk later," she said. We all lapsed into silence.

I was gazing at the passing traffic when the back of my neck prickled. I turned to look. A couple of tables away sat an old man with snow-white hair and dirty white kurta-pajamas. It took a split second to place him: He was the *same* guy from Sagar. The man poured tea into the saucer and slurped it unhurriedly, his black eyes studying me over the rim. In spite of the heat my arms were covered in goose bumps. An icy hand squeezed my heart. That crazy dude was stalking me and I was really creeped out. With a population of about fifty-four thousand (another little stat I'd found on Google), I'm sure there weren't many foreigners in Lolly-land. I must stand out like a scoop of vanilla ice cream in a chocolate sundae. I wondered if I should mention it to Mrs. Lal? Would she think I was paranoid? I wanted to catch Rohit's eye to ask if he'd noticed the old man but Rohit was studiously avoiding looking at me.

"There's Papa," said Rohit suddenly. He thumped his bottle on the table and stood up, his chair grating across the concrete floor. "Let's go."

Mrs. Lal paid for our drinks while I surreptitiously glanced at the old man. He was still staring at me. My heart lurched and I turned away. *He's just a stranger who's never seen a foreigner before, that's all.* The shopkeeper, a soccer ball with legs who reeked of curry, took our bill and money, all the while scratching his hair and showering his black kurta with dandruff. We hurried out of the shop while I tried to forget about the creepy Hannibal Lecter slash Saruman look-alike.

Rohit's dad, a slim, balding man with a slight stoop, crossed the road and hurried up to us. "Hello-*ji*," he said as he gave his wife a peck on her forehead. "Hi, Dylan. Enjoying Deolali?"

Up till a few days ago the trip had been awesome. It had gone steadily downhill since then but I wasn't going to say anything.

"It's been swag, Mr. Lal, thanks," I said, smiling. After years of practice, I'd become exceptionally good at hiding my feelings.

"And you, Rohit? Feels good to be home, doesn't it?" he said, thumping his son on the back.

Rohit gave an inaudible response. He acted tough with his mother but he didn't dare dis his dad. I was relieved Mr. Lal was here, but I had a terrible feeling that it was too late. Even if we made up, our friendship would never be the same again. Frodo and Sam had not endured.

"Ate those excellent *vadas* at Igatpuri station, Priya," Mr. Lal said. "*Oooof*, they were *too* good," he added, kissing his fingers with a loud smack. "And what delicious memories they brought back. Ahhh . . . too much!"

I smirked, knowing exactly what came next.

"Nothing in New York comes *close* to the taste of home," said Mr. Lal, shaking his head sorrowfully.

I snuck a glance at Rohit. We'd always laugh at this point in his dad's predictable lament but Rohit was looking straight ahead. My gut clenched. *Fine, two can play this game.*

"Let's go home, Arun," said Mrs. Lal. "I'll make tea while you have a shower. We have lots to discuss."

We hailed a scootie. I looked forward to another wild ride sans seat belt. The driver zoomed up and stopped in a cloud of dust.

"Where to?" he asked.

Mrs. Lal gave him our address, which, once again, I could barely pronounce let alone memorize.

"Get in," he said, turning the ancient meter to the right. "All of you."

"What?" said Mrs. Lal. "Are you mad?"

"Three in back and this *gora baba* in front," he said, pointing to me. "No problem!"

He wanted me to ride up front? And where was I supposed to sit? On the floor or on his lap? *Gross!*

"No way," Mrs. Lal and I said together.

She snapped her fingers at a passing scootie, which screeched to a halt millimeters away from her foot.

"Look where you're going, *pagal*," she yelled.

"Sorry, madam," said the second scootie driver, not looking the least bit sorry.

Mrs. Lal and I hopped into one. Rohit and his dad took the other.

Both drivers had, in an unspoken agreement, decided to race. We narrowly missed colliding with a cyclist transporting cages of screaming hens, a vendor with a tall stack of egg trays on the carrier behind him, and a lamppost. It was scary and thrilling all at once.

"Slow down," Mrs. Lal yelled at every turn. It had the reverse effect on the driver, who took it as an invitation to speed up. I grabbed the bar in front of me and hung on for dear life, imagining I was James Bond in a thrilling chase.

Finally the scootie stopped in front of our building in a choking cloud of dust. The driver's triumphant smile wilted as soon as he saw Mrs. Lal's expression.

"Why you angry, madam? I bring you triple-fast."

"*You jungli!* My heart almost stopped beating. Are you going to pay the bill if I have a heart attack? *Hunh?* Speak. *Speak!*"

The driver had the sense to shut up.

She paid the exact fare with not even one paisa as tip and marched into the building, her head held high. I followed at a slower pace and heard the driver mutter something very rude as he gunned the engine and sped off.

After we'd settled on the balcony with hot masala chai, Shrewsbury biscuits (similar to shortbread cookies), and sponge cake, we caught up on all the news about Nisha's wedding. According to Mr. Lal, who'd landed in Mumbai the day before, preparations were in full swing.

"And Anjali chewed up my ear about Rohit's behavior," said Mr. Lal. "What's all that about, *henh?*"

Rohit turned white. Mrs. Lal turned red. I almost choked on my biscuit.

"Let's go for a Hindi movie tonight," I blurted out. "It'll be fun."

"Here in Deolali?" asked Rohit, taking the bait just as I had hoped. "Are you crazy?"

"Yeah, why not?" I said, looking around at the Lals.

"For one, there are no subtitles," Rohit said coldly. "You'll be sitting through three hours of conversation that will make absolutely no sense to you."

"I'll figure it out," I replied. "If *I* don't have a problem, why should you?"

"And," continued Rohit as if I hadn't spoken at all, "the only theater here is old and has fans instead of air conditioners. If the electricity goes off, we'll be cooked. I'm not going."

"How often does that happen?" I said, recalling the power outage when we'd first arrived in Lolly-land. That one had barely lasted for thirty minutes and since then, luckily, it hadn't gone off once.

"Depends on how hot it gets and how many people turn on their air conditioners. The power supply in most cities, even small towns, cannot keep up with the demand when there's a heat wave," explained Mr. Lal. "So, there's a power shutdown throughout the city, in rotation, to try and balance out the usage. It's called load shedding and lasts a couple of hours. No big deal."

"Not even a fan for *two hours* in this intense heat would be brutal," I whispered, breaking out in a sweat just thinking about it.

172

"Welcome to India," said Rohit in a mocking tone. "You said this place was *hot* . . . Enjoy the heat."

"Oh come on, Rohit," said Mrs. Lal. "Stop being so negative! There's more to India than the heat!"

Rohit glared at her and she returned his gaze, unflinchingly. A storm was brewing and it wasn't over Mordor. It was in the Lals' apartment on their tiny balcony. Before I could say anything, Mrs. Lal spoke up.

"Boys, why don't you give us a few minutes?"

Rohit's mouth was a thin line and his twitching intensified. We both knew what this was about. I followed him as he marched inside and headed straight for the bedroom. He lay there on the bed, hands behind his head, staring unseeingly at the whitewashed ceiling.

"It's going to be okay, Ro."

He ignored me. With the mood he was in, there was no point trying to talk to him. I tiptoed back toward the living room. I could barely make out the murmur of voices from the balcony. I had to hear what they were saying. If I knew their plan, Rohit and I could form a counterplan.

I snuck a peek at Mr. and Mrs. Lal. They both had their backs to the living room. I hurried in and squeezed into the narrow gap between the sofa and the wall. Now I could hear them perfectly.

"I'm not disputing that Anjali's helped us a lot," Mrs. Lal was saying, "but I resent her bullying me with her money."

Just then I felt something behind me and almost yelled out

loud. I craned my neck to take a look. Rohit was beside me, finger to his lips. I nodded and continued with my eavesdropping.

"She only wants the best for us, Priya," said Mr. Lal.

"And the best thing for us is to have our family torn apart? Have you lost your mind, Arun?"

"No, dear, but—"

"This is blackmail, Arun. I will not stand for it and neither should you."

"What do you want me to do? My sister gave up her future to look after me. I owe her."

"You don't owe her your only child!" snapped Mrs. Lal. "Are you a man or a mouse?"

Before Mr. Lal could say a word, someone else did. The timing could not have been worse.

Squeak, squeak.

I whipped around to look at Rohit, wondering if he'd gone completely nuts. He pointed to something near the floor, a horrified look on his face. Just near the balcony door was a fist-size hole I hadn't noticed till now. A snout was just visible as the mouse sniffed the air and squeaked again, much louder than before.

SQUEAK, SQUEAK.

"How dare you boys hide here and make fun of me?" thundered Mr. Lal.

And there he was, glaring down at us still crouched behind the sofa but clearly visible. "Is this your idea of a joke, Rohit? And Dylan, I expected better of you."

"Papa, it wasn't us," said Rohit. "There really is a mouse."

But it was long gone, no doubt startled by Mr. Lal's yelling, and it had left us holding the cheese.

"Don't lie to me. I don't see anything. Maybe Anjali is right. You need to learn some manners and she's the best person for the job."

It was as if a depth charge had been set off in my stomach. "It's my fault, Mr. Lal. I wanted to know what was going on, so please don't take it out on Rohit."

Mr. Lal's expression softened slightly but he still looked mad and kind of embarrassed. Without a word he walked into his bedroom. Mrs. Lal followed him but not before we saw the disappointment on her face. Things were going from bad to worse. If I ever got my hands on that stupid mouse, I'd feed it to the crows.

After half an hour of complete silence, I couldn't take it anymore. Rohit and I had already had our fight and we were now in the cold war phase. His parents seemed to be in a similar situation.

"Why don't we all go to a movie tonight?" I said, rounding up the Lal family. "I'm sure we can figure this out in the morning. Please, Mr. Lal, spit out your anger."

I'd used the literal English translation of an Indian phrase I'd heard in a movie (Rohit had translated amid a lot of laughing at the time), hoping it would work. It did!

"Very well, Dylan," said Mr. Lal, a tiny smile on his face. "This is your vacation, too. We can eat out and then go for the movie at Malika Theater. We'll all be able to think clearly once we sleep on it."

"Don't expect too much from the theater," said Mrs. Lal. "It's quite basic."

"I won't," I said, not sure what she meant by *basic* aside from no air conditioning. I wondered if we'd have to take turns winding up the movie projector but, frankly, I didn't care. I might lose my best friend and had already lost my family. Things couldn't get worse.

I was so wrong.

FIFTEEN

W E TOOK A SCOOTIE TO THE BHEL HOUSE A SHORT while later. It was a tiny eatery with ten tables scrunched together, and the kitchen situated behind the pick-up counter. Rohit had been dragged there practically kicking and screaming and he was sulking.

"If Rohit doesn't want to go . . . maybe we should let him chill at home?" I'd asked. Time apart would probably be good for Rohit and his parents.

"Rubbish!" Mr. Lal said. "This is a family vacation and we will do *everything* as a family." After being compared to a mouse, Mr. Lal was overly forceful about making decisions, to get rid of the slightest doubt in anyone's mind about his masculinity.

"I'll wake you up when I'm going to the bathroom tomorrow morning," Rohit muttered. "We'll go together."

It earned him a glare from his parents.

I was really starting to appreciate my own parents. They'd never forced me to go anywhere with them. At the time I'd thought it was because they didn't love me enough, but I now realized they were respecting my boundaries. What a colossal dork I'd been! And with all of this melodrama going on, I'd forgotten to check my email. I made a mental note to do it as soon as we got home.

I tried the restaurant's signature dish—*bhel*—a concoction of puffed rice, fried vermicelli, potatoes, onions, and fresh cilantro mixed with sweet-and-sour chutney. The server combined all the ingredients in a large steel bowl and portioned it out into small white plates. He stuck a crisp *poori* on top and lined up the plates on the counter. Rohit's was the only dry one. No one wanted to go through the barfing incident again and the man had been warned to hold the chutney on Ro's portion.

We carried our plates to one of the empty tables. Mrs. Lal showed me how to scoop up the *bhel* with the *poori* and eat it Indian-style. I took a few pictures for my collection first, and then dug in. I crunched my way through it within minutes. It was good but nothing could erase the taste of loneliness from my mouth. I missed my friend.

"Good stuff, huh?" I asked. He'd been terribly quiet, his eyes glazed over except for the one time when he'd looked a little panicked as he groped for something in his pockets. When Mrs. Lal asked him if everything was all right, he'd nodded. But I knew him well enough to figure out something was wrong. I also guessed he didn't want his parents to know, so I decided to ask him when we were alone.

"It's not bad," said Rohit politely. He continued to shovel *bhel* into his mouth automatically and declined seconds.

With dinner over, I couldn't wait to get to the movie and forget my problems for a few hours. The vendors' carts lining the street were lit by kerosene lamps that attracted clouds of suicidal insects, dashing against the hot glass and dying on contact.

The air was hot and thick, with a patchwork of dark clouds covering the sky. Now and then thunder rumbled overhead and I hoped for a downpour to cool off this sauna of a place.

As we ambled along the main street, I gazed at the gigantic movie posters on the billboards and walls. Without exception, every poster had an evil villain, a curvy beauty, and a smiling hero in a flamboyant outfit.

"So, Dylan, which movie do you want to see?" asked Mr. Lal.

"This one," I said, pointing to a particularly gory poster that prominently featured a graveyard. "They've misspelled *booth*."

"That's *bhooth*," said Mr. Lal. "It means 'ghost.'"

"Like it already," I said, flicking up my thumb.

Rohit rolled his eyes but said nothing. Mr. Lal bought tickets and we walked into the dingy cavern of the theater along with hordes of other people. The smells of sweat and stale popcorn swirled thickly around us but by now I was used to it. Only two movies were playing at this theater, rather than the ten to sixteen movies at the multiplex cinemas back home.

We found seats at the back of the hall, bathed in dim yellow lights. The ads had started and I plunked down on my seat only to leap up immediately.

"Arrrghh," I said, trying not to yell.

"Dylan?" said Mrs. Lal. "What's the matter?"

"Something in that seat is trying to get out," I squeaked. Visions of the humongous rat we'd seen outside Rohit's flat in Mumbai, and the mouse at the Lolly-land flat, flashed through my mind.

"Only the springs," said Mrs. Lal. "This theater is old and will be shut down soon. I've heard a new one will be built by the end of the year but for now this is it. Rohit, change seats with Dylan, please. After all, he is your guest."

"Not a chance," said Rohit. "My bottom has less padding than his."

Even in the gloom, Mrs. Lal's glare was unmistakable. "Take my seat, Dylan. Or maybe we can find better ones, Arun?"

"The place is full and there aren't any more decent seats left," said Mr. Lal, craning his neck to look around. "We'll have to manage with these."

"It's okay, Mrs. Lal," I replied quickly before another argument broke out. "I'll just sit to one side. It's not so bad."

In fact it *sucked*! Scratchy seat guts rubbed against my thigh and the metal spring pushed against my butt, desperate to escape. But it was these seats or sit right up front with our noses touching the screen. I ground my teeth and tried to ignore the discomfort as the lights went out and the trailers began.

More people trickled in, laughing and talking loudly. The fans set along the walls were completely ineffective and, as promised, there was no air-conditioning. The temperature in the theater climbed steadily. The spring under my bottom seemed even more determined to get out. I was so hot, I was sure I'd have melted away by the time the movie ended. I realized, too late, that Rohit had been absolutely right. If we weren't fighting, I would have listened to him instead of suffering through the terrible theater conditions. But the alternative was to go back to the flat and mope. *Not. Happening.*

"We can still walk out if you like," Mr. Lal said, glancing at Mrs. Lal vigorously fanning herself with a newspaper. She never left home without one and now I knew why. Rohit sat glowering, his face shiny with sweat.

"Yes, please let's get out," said Rohit. "I can't stand this heat any longer."

"It's not so bad," said Mrs. Lal. "And we've paid so much money for the tickets—" She stopped abruptly as Mr. Lal put a hand on her knee, his eyes flicking toward me.

A hot flush crept up my neck. I had *asked* to come. And now I wanted them to leave because of an uncomfortable seat and the heat. I felt terrible making them waste their hard-earned money, especially since it was causing so much tension already. I knew they'd never let me repay them.

"Why don't we take a vote?" I asked. "I'll do whatever the majority wants." This way the decision wouldn't be entirely mine and I wouldn't feel too guilty.

"We leave," said Rohit promptly. His eyes caught mine in a warning glare. *Now* he wanted me to side with him after butting heads all night. *Not a chance, bud.*

"I'd like to stay," said Mrs. Lal.

"I'll go with what my wife wants," said Mr. Lal. "Stay."

Crap! That left me with the final vote. "I'd like to stay, too," I said.

Rohit's eyes burned brighter than the Eye of Sauron. Then he looked away without saying a word.

I squirmed in the seat to get comfortable but it was a lost cause. I reminded myself—I was a New Yorker. We could survive anything!

The movie started and I sat back to enjoy it. The title burst onto the screen accompanied by eerie music. As the camera zoomed in on a girl being strangled to death, the heat and the spring warring with my butt faded away momentarily. Hoots and catcalls peppered the air. It was easy to follow the story even though I didn't understand a word. The crying scenes got a bit tedious because everyone sobbed buckets, *all the time.*

Barely ten minutes into the movie, the hero burst into a song. Clapping echoed around the room. The heroine danced around a tree in the rain, singing melodiously all the while.

"Man, these songs make no sense at all," I whispered to Rohit, unable to stop myself. "And they're a real pace-killer. If Sam and Frodo had frolicked around the bushes with the elves every half hour, each of the *Lord of the Rings* and *Hobbit* movies would be six hours long. Thank God Peter Jackson, not an Indian director, made them!"

Not a word from El Groucho by my side.

Just as the song was coming to an end, the image on the screen wobbled and went fuzzy for an instant. The temperature rose. I was glued to my seat with sweat. The Lals would have to scrape me off when it was time to go. The image shuddered again. A prickle of fear started at the base of my neck and crept toward my extremities. Something was wrong.

Suddenly the electricity went off, *even the emergency exit lights*. The darkness was so complete I couldn't see my hand in front of my face. Hoots and shouts echoed from every corner of the theater as the audience demanded a refund. My heart pounded. I couldn't breathe.

"Power outage?" I asked, trying to keep my voice from trembling. I needed to say something, *anything*, or I'd start screaming for help.

"Yes," Mrs. Lal said, affirming the obvious. "Let's all stay calm."

"I told you we shouldn't have come," snapped Rohit. "But does anyone listen to me? *No!* You all listen to this idiot who doesn't have a clue about a movie theater in a small town in India."

"That's enough, Rohit," his dad snapped. "We're here now and there's nothing we can do. The lights should be back any moment now."

Five scorching minutes limped by. Nothing happened. Around us people shifted and chattered as if they were quite used to it. Wanting to get their money's worth, I guessed, most stayed in their seats. I wanted to get out, like, last year.

"Arun, we should leave," said Mrs. Lal in a shaky voice. "It's taking too long. I think something's wrong."

"Relax," said Mr. Lal. "In India everything takes time."

I squeezed my eyes shut, rested my head against the back of the seat, and took deep breaths. Not again, *never again* would I insist on doing something I had been warned against. This was my punishment for not listening to Ro. I'd get down on my knees and apologize to him if only the electricity would come back on, or if we could escape this stinking darkness.

And then someone yelled out a word that had exactly the same reaction around the world.

"AAG!" *Fire!*

SIXTEEN

MY HEART STUTTERED. I GRABBED THE ARMRESTS as the world around me spun crazily. A sudden flash of orange light from the back of the theater illuminated hundreds of heads turned toward it. Smoke and flames crackled behind the glass plate of the projector room and it shattered. Agonized yells erupted and the stampede began.

"Run!" Mr. Lal yelled.

We ran toward the exits. People hurtled past, trampling our feet, climbing over seats, *over us,* in their hurry to get out. I yelled in pain as someone elbowed my stomach but no one was listening. Everyone was too busy trying to escape. Rough hands pinched and pushed and grasped in the darkness while the ominous orange light grew steadily brighter, and the theater became a furnace.

"Dylan, Rohit, stay together!" shouted Mrs. Lal. Her fingers dug into my shoulder with a reassuring ferocity.

The stench of smoke and burning plastic started to fill the room. The smell was so foul, I could barely breathe. I gasped for air. There seemed to be none.

"Whose *brilliant* idea was this?" snarled Rohit as we were pushed along with the crowd. But under that anger was deep fear. "Dylan, when we get out of this mess, I'm going to kill you."

I didn't bother to answer. Instead I grabbed his arm as we ran toward the exit, trying not to stumble over seats and other people. I could only think about getting out into the open where I could draw a lungful of clean air.

Shadows converged at a door that had been forced open. Someone shoved me hard and I went down. Feet pummeled my head as people climbed over me, not bothering to see what or who they were running over. I screamed but it was drowned out by hundreds of panicked cries. I tried to get up but the tidal wave of people kept coming. Everything around me started to dim and I fought to stay conscious. If I fainted, that was the end of Dylan Moore.

"Rohit, I fell," I yelled out with everything I had. "HELP!" Even as I called out his name I had a horrible feeling he'd ignore me. Our friendship was over. Why would he bother to save me?

I don't know how, but Rohit heard me. *Through all that commotion, my bud heard me and came back.*

"Where are you?" Rohit yelled. "Keep talking!"

"Here, on the floor," I called out. Something furry brushed past my face. Rats!

Rohit shouted at people in Hindi, his voice drawing closer. I fought to sit upright, waving my hand in the air. Finally his hand clasped mine and he hauled me to my feet. I almost bawled right there.

"Run, Dylan, this place could go up in flames any minute," he said in a choked voice. "I didn't see any fire extinguishers."

Dripping with sweat and gasping for air, we ran like a couple of crazed animals escaping a forest fire. "Where are your parents?" I asked.

"They must be ahead. Keep going!" said Rohit.

We were swept along with the crowd. I came close to losing my balance again but grabbed someone's shirt to stay on my feet. There was a lot of shoving and punching and for once I gave back as good as I got without feeling guilty. I knew if I went down one more time, I wasn't getting back up.

"Don't you dare fall again," said Rohit, echoing my thoughts. "You'll be trampled to death." His face was close to mine and twisted with fear.

"Yeah, I know," I said. I was so tightly wedged in the crowd, I couldn't breathe. My legs were like rubber and my heart was ready to call it a day. Fear kept me going. I didn't want to die—not here and not today.

At last we were out in the open. The crush of sweaty bodies eased a bit. I sucked in a lungful of night air. It was tinged with the smell of burning wood and something so foul, I gagged.

Around me, all of Lolly-land was dark. I guessed the power outage must have shorted something at the decrepit theater and caused the fire. Someone had placed kerosene lamps along the road so we could see where we were going.

More people poured out of the theater as we moved farther away. Orange flames leaped out from a hole in the roof and the thought of being trapped inside made me retch. Shrieks of pain and anger and panic filled the air as parents looked for their children, wives for their husbands, and lost kids for a familiar face. Rats in every shape and size scurried for cover. I coughed and gasped, trying to get the smoke out of my lungs.

"Now we've got to find Ma and Papa," said Rohit, scanning the crowd.

In the light of the lanterns he looked small and scared. Grimy streaks crisscrossed his face, and his T-shirt had torn in several places in the struggle to get out. I looked down and realized I didn't look much better, though thankfully I hadn't lost my camera. And we were *alive*. Now all we had to do was find Rohit's parents and go home.

"I'm sure they're looking for us, too," I said. "Let's walk around a bit." Neither of us said the one thing that made me want to barf just thinking about it.

The fire department arrived. Even before the truck rolled to a stop, men jumped out with hoses and started spraying the remains of the theater still being devoured by flames. Shortly after, the ambulances and police arrived. Paramedics tended to the people who'd inhaled the most smoke, while the police kept the crowds away and told those who were unharmed to clear the area. Unfortunately curious passersby had now gathered and the crowd around the theater swelled.

Thunder and lightning lit up the sky. I prayed for rain to douse the smoldering wreckage.

I drew in a deep, shaky breath, staring at the ruined shell that had been a theater less than an hour before. We'd been incredibly lucky to get out alive and unharmed. I refused to let myself think about what might have happened if Rohit hadn't come back for me. We wove through the crowd, calling out for the Lals. There was no reply.

We grabbed a passing paramedic. "Please, have you seen my parents?" Rohit blurted out.

"Let me talk," I said, squeezing his shoulder. I quickly described the Lals and what they were wearing. "Have you seen them?"

The young paramedic shook his head. "Sorry, no, but three ambulances answered the emergency call. You can check with the others."

We did. No one had seen them.

"What if they . . ." Rohit started to say. He gulped and stopped, his lower lip trembling.

"Don't be an idiot, Ro. They were ahead of us. I'm sure they got out. They're somewhere around looking for us just like we're looking for them."

We wandered for another half hour, circling the theater, calling out their names, grabbing policemen and pedestrians, describing them till we were hoarse. No one had seen them and no one replied to our calls. A cold hand squeezed my heart as reality started to sink in. Suppose they hadn't managed to escape? Rohit must have reached the same conclusion because he suddenly whirled on me.

"This is *your* fault!" he snarled, tears coursing down his face. He didn't even bother to wipe them away. "If you hadn't insisted on watching a movie, we'd still be at home. Ma and Papa would have been safe and alive."

"My fault?" I snapped. I was so angry and scared, I could barely speak. "Did it occur to you that I could have died in there, too?"

"Yeah, and I came back to save you when I should have made sure my parents were safe. And now they're gone. Yes, it's *all* your fault. I *hate* you, Dylan Moore."

I knew he was upset and scared. I understood what he was going through, and yet his words were a knife in my gut.

I'd never felt so betrayed or utterly alone in my life.

SEVENTEEN

ROHIT AND I CIRCLED THE THEATER THREE MORE times. There was no sign of Mr. and Mrs. Lal. Each time we completed a round, Rohit's mouth would crumple and I'd suggest we go again.

"Maybe they've been taken to the hospital?" I asked, noticing the flashing lights of a departing ambulance.

"You think they're so badly hurt they're in the hospital?" he asked, his arms twitching at his sides as if he were a malfunctioning robot. And even though I was mad at him, I felt his panic. What if they were my parents? I pushed the thought away. Right now I had to focus on Mrs. Lal, drill sergeant slash caring mom; Mr. Lal, Gandhi incarnate with a dry sense of humor; and my best friend. The Lals were my second family. I couldn't rest till I knew they were all okay.

"People are hospitalized even for smoke inhalation," I said. "I'm *sure* they're all right, Ro, and probably worried sick about *us* right now."

"You're absolutely right," he said. "Yes, that's it!" He nodded so vigorously his glasses fell off his nose and bounced on the pavement. He stooped to grab them and only when he put them back on with shaking fingers did he realize the right lens was cracked.

"Just great," he said in a tired voice. "Blind in one eye."

"Let's go home," I said. "It's no use hanging around here." The fire had died away but the remains of the theater still belched thick black smoke. The crowds had almost dispersed and the firemen were packing up their gear.

"Always thinking about yourself, aren't you?" snapped Rohit. "How can we go home when my parents are missing?"

"I *meant* in order to check if they're already there and then go to a hospital or police station," I said, my anger starting to simmer again. "I'm sure your mom will expect us to use common sense."

Stay cool. I had to repeat it to myself like a mantra. *Panic and fear are making him say these cruel things. He can't mean it.* But I couldn't help wondering if this was what he really thought of me. Had our friendship been so weak that at the first sign of trouble it had fallen apart? Or had this trip shown us that we'd never really been best friends in the first place? I understood, now, what Ron might have felt when he thought Harry had entered the Triwizard Tournament without telling him.

"They could be walking around the theater in the same direction and might be ahead, or behind us," said Rohit, trying to reason it out. "That's why we haven't bumped into them. Right? *Right?*"

"We've gone around a bunch of times, in both directions. They're definitely not here," I said. "They could be anywhere. So, we check the flat, then the hospital, and then the police station. And then we do it again."

"I say we stay right here," said Rohit. "Mom wouldn't leave till she'd found us."

Arguing, we moved away from the theater and turned onto a quieter street. A few beggars slept on, oblivious or unconcerned about the chaos just around the corner. The air was hot and stifling. I was so drained I thought I would pass out right there.

"So what do we do?" I asked.

Rohit started walking. I hoped it was toward the flat because I had no idea where we were. And I definitely couldn't remember the flat's address.

Suddenly a movement caught my eye. I whipped around. Shadows flickered but no one was there. The power had come back on but the streetlights were so dim, they barely illuminated the road. I fell into step beside Rohit, my heart pounding. The hair on the back of my neck prickled. Someone was following us. I knew it. Felt it.

"Call them on your cell!" I said in a flash of inspiration. I couldn't *believe* neither of us had thought of it earlier. My memory lapse probably had to do with my smoke-addled brain and sheer panic. One call would solve all our problems!

Rohit gave me a sheepish look. "I already thought of it."

"So then what are you waiting for?" I yelled. "The return of the king?"

"Forgot the cell phone at home when I plugged it in to charge," mumbled Rohit, not meeting my gaze. He took off his glasses and rubbed his eyes. "I remembered during dinner but since we were all together, I figured . . ." His voice trailed away. "If I'd told Ma I'd forgotten it at home she would have ripped me apart and made us go back for it. Now I wish I had. And then we would have missed the movie and we wouldn't be going through this nightmare."

So *that* explained the momentary panic at dinner. "How could you be so *stupid*?" I hissed. "Back home the cell is glued to your fingers. And you forget it when we need it the most?"

"Then why didn't *you* carry one?" asked Rohit. "I'm sure your parents could have afforded to give you a cell phone with a local phone plan, *moron*!"

He had a point there. They'd offered, insisted even, but I'd refused. I wanted to get away from everything completely even if it was only for three weeks. I didn't want Mom and Dad calling me with endless advice or complaints about each other and had asked them to email me instead. And now my plan had backfired.

"Do you at least know the way home?" I asked.

"It was saved on my phone but I know it's in Deolali Camp and starts with a *G*," he said.

"Brilliant!" I said. "Starts with a *G* . . . should be good enough for a scootie driver."

"There's no need to be sarcastic," he snapped. "Do *you* remember it?"

"No, because I don't live here. I'm just visiting."

"It's been five years since I've been back to Deolali!" said Rohit in a squeaky voice.

"Oi, *chup karo*," someone muttered close by. "We're trying to sleep."

We stood under a lamppost, glaring at each other. I was so mad at Rohit, I couldn't speak. His sweaty face mirrored my frustration and anger. *I* had suggested we go to the movie but it was *his* fault for forgetting to bring his phone or memorizing his home address. Six of one and half a dozen of the other, as Mom loved to say. *Now what?*

"Let's go find a phone booth and call them," said Rohit.

"Great idea," I said. It was the first smart thing he'd said all night. "I have lots of change."

"You are lost," said a gruff voice behind me. "Need help?"

I whirled around, unintentionally grabbing Rohit's arm so tight he yelped. A man limped out from the shadows. He was dressed in shabby clothes that stank even from a distance. In spite of the heat, he wore a floppy hat. Eyebrows like white caterpillars hung over deep black eyes that bored into us. My heart went into shock and the rest of me wanted to follow. Sam was tougher than Frodo, I reminded myself. *Try not to faint, please.*

"No, thank you," Rohit managed to squeak. "We were on our way home."

"But I think you are looking for *Ma* and *Papa*," he said, imitating Rohit with uncanny accuracy. "And you have no cell phone."

Slowly he slipped his cap off, revealing snow-white hair. It felt as if I'd plunged into a pool on a winter morning. This was the *same* man we'd seen at Sagar and then again at the tea stall. My stalker had caught up with me at the worst possible time.

"You've been following me, you perv!" I yelled, trying to keep my voice steady. "Just leave us alone."

"I see you run from fire," he said softly. "Take you home where it's safe. Come."

He seemed to speak English decently enough but his tone and mannerisms seemed a bit off. My brain was bouncing around my skull on high alert.

He shuffled closer, clutching a tattered umbrella in one hand. His other hand reached out for us, yellow fingernails encrusted with dirt. We backed away.

"Come with me," he repeated.

Rohit and I exchanged glances. I wasn't walking as far as the next lamppost with this weirdo, let alone home.

"No, thank you," said Rohit, sharply. "We know the way."

The man stared at us with those piercing eyes. I looked around for help. All the shops were shut and no one was in sight. Mrs. Lal wasn't kidding when she said this small town went to sleep early. Now it was just us and this whacko in the dead of night. We had no phone and neither of us knew the way home. The seriousness of the situation crashed over me like a tsunami.

"Really?" the old man whispered. Just the way he said it made my skin crawl.

He smiled. I swear the resemblance to Hannibal slash Saruman was uncanny. Before my legs turned to jelly and became completely useless, I grabbed Rohit's arm. "Run!" I yelled.

And then we were running down the street for our lives. Hands clasped tight, we zipped in and out of the shadows. The last time I'd held hands with anyone in public was when I was a toddler, but if I let go, I wouldn't have the strength to run at all. Rohit was the only thing keeping me on my feet for the second time that night.

Up ahead, the streetlight was off. Darkness loomed. We kept running. Horrible thoughts pounded my head as our feet pounded the asphalt. What if we were kidnapped and I never saw my mom again? What if this psycho decided to snack on our limbs? What if this madman killed us and sold our body parts on the black market? I'd seen that in a movie one time. And why had I been dumb enough to watch so many horror movies when Mom had told me not to?

Note to Self: There's a reason why some movies are rated R. Remembering the horrible ways you could die might slow you down when you're actually *running for your life. From now on you're only watching Disney movies!*

A rhythmic slap-slap sound followed us down the street. We stopped. The footsteps stopped. Loud panting filled the air. "Don't run, my dears," the old man pleaded.

"This way," hissed Rohit and we darted into a side street.

We were so lost we didn't care where we went as long as we could get away from our stalker. The creepy music from *Psycho*, when Norman Bates stabs a woman taking a shower, pulsed through my mind. I almost stumbled and fell. *Stop thinking about horror movies and focus!*

Thump, thump, thump. Us running down the road.

Slap, slap, slap. Psycho in slippers following us.

Squee, squee, squee, squee. Psycho soundtrack echoing in my head.

I ran faster, dragging Rohit with me. The old man sure had stamina; he was still right behind us. He must want to kill us really badly. My legs suddenly shot out from under me and I landed on my butt with a resounding thud.

"Ow-ow, OWW!"

"Shut up," growled Rohit, yanking me to my feet. "Can't you yell quietly?"

I refused to answer as I got to my feet and hobbled after him, my backside throbbing. Ro and I realized, at the same instant, what a huge mistake we'd made. The side street we'd turned onto led to a dead-end alley. We whirled to run back out when a dark shadow fell across the entrance.

I clutched Rohit's hand, murmuring, "Our Lord who art in heaven . . ."

"*Om Namah Shivaya . . .*" Rohit muttered under his breath.

Hoping the double whammy of prayers to Jesus and a powerful (I hoped!) Hindu god would save us, we inched backward, staring at the growing shadow. I looked behind us, but the wall was at least six feet high. Even with a ladder, I'd have had difficulty *climbing* over. Vaulting over was totally out of the question. Ditto for Rohit. We were trapped! Every horror movie I'd ever seen flashed through my mind. Dismembered body parts and lots of blood . . .

The geezer inched closer. His black eyes locked with mine.

I wondered how I'd taste, pickled in formaldehyde.

Squee, squee, squee, SQUEEE.

EIGHTEEN

IN THE DIM LIGHT OF THE LONE STREETLAMP, THE old man sidled even closer. I could feel his malevolent gaze and smell his decaying body. Sweat trickled down my back. I glanced at Rohit. He had a determined look on his sweat-slicked face. His elbows jabbed his sides rapidly, as if he were winding up for takeoff. The eye staring out of the shattered lens of his glasses was trained on Psycho.

"Should we rush forward and knock him over?" I whispered. False bravado. My knees were knocking so much I could barely stand, let alone run.

"We can try," said Rohit.

"Wait, I have an idea," I said. I slipped the Rolex off my wrist and clasped it tightly, waiting for the right moment.

"I don't think—" Rohit started to say but I shushed him.

"A Rolex doesn't just tell time, it tells history. Anyone can appreciate that."

I waited till the old guy was close enough and threw my watch at him. It bounced off his nose and landed on the ground with a sharp crack that echoed in my heart.

"*That* is a Rolex," I said, trying to keep my voice steady. "It might be scratched now but even so you'll get a very good price for it. Just leave us alone, er . . . *sir.*"

The man grimaced and rubbed his nose, emitting a low growl. He didn't try to pick up the watch. I knew then we were in *serious* trouble. He wanted us, not our valuables. This was no petty thief, but a serial killer. Why didn't I buy pepper spray when I'd first noticed this psycho at Sagar? I could have emptied the can in his face, saved my Rolex, and we'd be on our way home. Visions of the blood-splattered sidewalks flashed through my mind. I had been *dying* to see a murder and now I was going to see one—mine!

"You *idiot*," whispered Rohit. "At least you could have thrown the watch at his feet. Now we have an angry old psycho."

"Crap," I whispered.

"You want money, we'll give you money," said Rohit. "I have lots of it at home. Just take us there and you can have it all."

"Don't need money . . . I just want my kids back," he said, his voice breaking.

My bowels were liquefying along with the rest of me and I was in real danger of peeing my pants. "And our moms want *us* back," I said, trying to reason with him. "Please let us go, sir, and we'll help you find your kids."

"Too late for that now," he replied. "You're all I have, all I want."

"We are so dead," I whispered. In utter frustration I yelled, *"Jao!"*

Creepy smile from Psycho.

Rohit glanced at me. Then he swallowed and stepped in front of me, shielding me with his body. "This is my friend, sir, and a *guest* in our country. You will not harm him. If you let him go, I'll come with you quietly."

For a moment I was so shocked I could only stare at the back of his large head. After the horrible things we'd said to each other just a few minutes ago, I was sure he'd want to ditch me. But here he was trying to protect me (even though it would have taken three of him to protect me properly). Could I have been utterly wrong about our friendship? Did I have it in me to be as brave as he was? There was a lump the size of a golf ball in my throat and my eyes became strangely watery.

"You will let us *both* go, sir!" I said, stepping up to stand next to Rohit. "Or I'll knock your head off. I'm a black-belt Karate Kid . . ." I took up the classic stance: knees bent, turning sideways, and trying to imitate the kick I'd seen the Kid do in the movie. I overbalanced and Rohit had to grab my T-shirt so I wouldn't keel over and fall flat on my face.

"You better watch out!" I said, putting my fists up in front of my face. "These babies are lethal." I jabbed the air a couple of times to let him know I meant business. "You come any closer and you'll be kissing this," I said, waving my fist at him.

"Come home with me, my sweeties," he said, shuffling closer. "Daddy only wants to tell you a story. You loved hearing about Hanuman, the Monkey God, destroying Lanka. Remember?"

All of Mom's warnings about talking to strangers or going anywhere with them echoed in my head. *Sorry, daddy-o, but these sweeties aren't going anywhere with you. And I don't like monkeys.*

"An invisibility cloak would be so useful right about now," moaned Rohit. "Or a large rock."

"As long as we have each other, we don't need anything else," I said. And I meant it.

The old man slipped his hand into his tattered jacket and my heart almost burst out of my chest. I had to do something. Fast. I remembered the camera around my neck.

"When I give the signal, run," I whispered to Rohit, tapping my camera lightly. Rohit glanced at me and nodded.

The old man shuffled closer. Not breaking eye contact with him, I switched on the camera and set off the flash in a burst of blinding light. The old man instinctively raised his hand to cover his eyes.

"CHARGE!" I yelled and ran straight at him. I shoved him hard and so did Rohit. He fell over like a bowling pin. Then we were running out of the alley as fast as our shaky legs could carry us, the camera thumping on my chest.

The old man recovered quickly and within seconds he was on his feet and pursuing us, grunting ominously and muttering in Hindi.

We raced out of the alley and turned right. The street was deserted and behind us the footsteps grew louder. I grasped Rohit's slick hand in mine as we ran.

"Someone help us!" I called out.

"Please, HELP!" Rohit echoed.

"In here, quick," said a voice. A hand shot out of an open doorway and beckoned.

Without further hesitation we dived into a dimly lit hovel, one of many that lined the street. As soon as we raced in, the door swung shut and the light went out. My nose was assaulted by a dank, musty smell. We heard the old man cursing as he approached the huts. Then nothing.

"Where are you?" The gruff voice pierced the silence. He was right outside and I almost started crying. If he decided to fling open the door, we were dead. I was so winded I couldn't even stand, let alone run. My life sped up in my mind's eye. *Goodbye, world!*

"I just want to talk to you," the man whispered, a sob in his voice. "I promise you."

Rohit squeezed my hand tight and I squeezed back as I tried to slow my breathing.

Just then there was a tremendous crack, as if Thor's hammer had shattered the sky. The heavens opened up and rain pounded the pavement. Thank God. No one could be crazy enough to look for us in a downpour. Not even Psycho!

For five agonizing minutes we sat in the murky darkness while my eyes adjusted to the surroundings. Then it hit me: We'd escaped Psycho but who would we find in the room with us when the lights came on again?

NINETEEN

THE RANK ODOR IN THE ROOM LESSENED SLIGHTLY as someone cracked open the door. I heard something scrape against a rough surface again and again. The only image that came to mind was a blunt instrument being sharpened. For a kill.

"Be ready to run," whispered Rohit.

"'Kay," I said. My heart objected strenuously to being put through so much in so short a time but I told it to stuff it.

A match flared and what seemed like a disembodied hand lit the wick of a kerosene lamp in the center of the room. Soft golden light lit up the face of our savior. I slumped back in relief.

An ancient woman (she looked at least five hundred years old!) in a tattered saree, so faded I couldn't even make out the color, smiled at us. Her sharp black eyes crinkled at the corners, and toothless gums peeked out from between her wrinkled lips.

"I'm Rohit . . . Thank you for saving us."

"Namaste!" I said. "I'm Dylan."

The woman nodded. "I'm Shakuntala," she said in a slightly indistinct voice. She was so thin and frail; I couldn't believe she lived in a tiny shack. She should have been in a nice, comfortable home surrounded by nurses and other ancient people.

"Who was that psycho chasing us?" I asked.

"That was Rafiq," she said. "He lost his wife and two boys in an accident many years ago."

"But why was he chasing *us*?" I said. "He's been stalking me since I got here."

The old woman sat down on her makeshift bed and leaned against the wall, sighing deeply. "Whenever he sees two boys together it triggers something in his mind—he goes a little mad."

"He should be locked up, Aunty," I said. "He chased us and almost gave me a heart attack."

She laughed. "Rafiq looks scary but really, he's harmless. He *was* telling the truth when he said he only wanted to talk. He would have made you listen to a story and let you go. No harm done."

"So, if he's harmless, why didn't you come out and *talk* to him?" I said. "Why hide us?"

"When he's in this excitable state, it's hard to reason with him," said Shakuntala. "It's best to stay out of his way. He'll be all right by tomorrow."

Rohit and I exchanged glances. Crap. Had we just escaped a madman to get stuck with a batty woman? *Dear Lord who art in heaven . . .* I'd forgotten what came next but I hoped the Good Lord wouldn't hold it against me.

"We're going to contact the police tomorrow morning," I said firmly. "He should not be allowed to roam the streets."

Shakuntala looked at me calmly. "The police will beat him up and release him. Once he's on the street, he'll do it again. The fear of being beaten up will not stop him from missing his boys. Is that what you want?"

I remembered the bruise on Psycho's cheek I'd noticed at Sagar. My resolve weakened a little but I still wasn't convinced. "Why don't they put him into a hospital and treat him? Why let him run around terrorizing people?"

"Son," said Shakuntala, "India has over a billion people and not enough money to look after them all. The hospitals and asylums are overrun with the worst cases and even then there's a waitlist. Rafiq won't even qualify. Why don't you just forgive and forget? Sometimes it's the only thing in your control."

Easy for her to say. She wasn't chased by a psycho in the middle of the night and aged ten years in ten minutes.

"You are welcome to spend the night in my home," she said. "It's not fancy but it's fairly dry and you'll be safe."

I let my eyes travel around the one-room hovel. It had a few blackened, dented pots in a corner. On a line strung across the back of the room were a few ragged bits of clothing. In another corner were piles of rags, empty plastic jugs, and lots of aluminum cans of every shape, size, and color. The place smelled strongly of kerosene oil, sweat, and mud. But we *were* safe and at the moment I didn't care if it smelled like cow dung. Now and then a drop of water would land on my head. I looked up and was shocked at the state of the damp ceiling covered with ugly water marks and holes. The grimy windows filtered the light from the streetlamps, making the room dark.

"We have to get back," said Rohit. "There was a fire at the theater. We got separated from our parents." His voice faltered and I squeezed his arm. "I have to know if they are all right."

"Not tonight," she said. "You won't find a scootie at this hour in the rain. Do you want to walk there?"

Rohit and I exchanged glances. Rafiq loomed large in my mind, and harmless or not, I wasn't ready for another encounter. Not. Happening.

"No," I said. "But we have to leave as soon as it's light and the rain stops."

"All right," she said. "But, while you are here, you can help me catch the leaks."

The kerosene lamp was strategically situated in the one place where the roof didn't leak. After we spread out all the pots and pans to catch the drips, we sat down again, facing each other. All the running around had made me hungry and my stomach growled.

"Sorry," I said, clutching the culprit, hoping it wouldn't embarrass me again.

"Come, you must eat a bite with me," Shakuntala said. "After all, you are my guests."

"Thank—" I started to say when Rohit cut in with a quick frown.

"No, er . . . we're too stuffed," said Rohit. "But thank you for asking."

"Nonsense," she said. "I'm a poor woman but what is mine is yours." She glanced at Rohit, her lined face crinkling into a smile. It was like watching ripples on a pond, and just as calming. "In India, a guest is like a god and should be treated like one. No?"

I turned to Rohit. "I'm your god . . . *cool!* Why didn't you ever tell me?"

His glare was enough to silence me immediately.

Shakuntala shuffled over to a corner of the room that must have been her kitchen and brought out two dented tin plates. "You two can share one. Moti and I will share the other."

"Moti?" I said, looking around. How could I have missed seeing anyone else in this tiny place? Was it her husband? And if so, was he hiding under the pile of garbage? Because there was no other place he could be.

"My friend and companion," she replied with a smile.

"Uh-huh," said Rohit, looking around the room. "Where is he?"

"Oh he'll come and greet you when the food's on the plate," she said, laughing. "He's a greedy little pig."

I hoped her husband was a nice guy. I could only imagine Dad's face if Mom ever described him as a "greedy little pig" in front of strangers.

Shakuntala took the lid off a small copper pot. I was so hungry I was willing to eat a snake or a frog as long as it was well cooked and spicy. At the bottom of the pot were a couple of handfuls of rice mixed with some kind of green vegetable. She ladled out the food onto each plate, piling a bit more into one. Then Shakuntala took a tiny red onion from a basket, peeled it, and smashed it with the heel of her palm, adding a few bits to both plates. The pungent fumes made my eyes water but I kept my mouth shut.

She held out the larger portion to us. "Enjoy."

I stared at it and then at Rohit, speechless. His eyes glinted with moisture. I knew, without a doubt, we were thinking the same thing. This was her dinner. Probably breakfast, too. But she was willing to share it with complete strangers. This would never happen back home, where most people wouldn't give you the time of day let alone their next meal.

"Er . . . thank you, Aunty," said Rohit. "But we had a huge meal before the movie and we aren't hungry at all."

"Not at all," I echoed him. I like to think she would have believed me but my stomach had a mind of its own. It rumbled loudly in protest again at that precise moment.

"I know liars when I see them," she said, smiling. "My own children lied to me often. Please eat! I know it's not much but at least hunger will not be gnawing at your stomachs tonight."

We sat on the mud floor, facing Shakuntala. She didn't give us any cutlery and I watched Rohit hesitate for a minute before picking up a morsel of food using his hand, the way his mom ate. I did the same, and even though I dropped most of it through my awkwardly clenched fingers, it was strangely satisfying to feel the texture of the food before putting it into my mouth.

Moti made an appearance at last. He'd been hiding in the garbage pile after all. He crawled out, stretched, and walked toward us, sniffing the air—a black-and-white mongrel with spindly legs and a torn ear. He came to Shakuntala and nudged her gently. She stroked his nose while she murmured something in Hindi to him. And then she did something that made my throat close and tears prick the backs of my eyes.

Out of the tiny portion on her plate, she pushed a little to one side. Moti started licking his portion without encroaching on hers. It was clear they had eaten like this before.

My skin tingled. I abandoned my meal, wiped my hands on my shorts, and raised the camera, knowing with utter certainty that this was The Picture. *This* was what I had been searching for all along. It captured the essence of friendship like nothing else had on my entire trip.

"Eat, child," Shakuntala said. "You can take pictures later. Moti and I are going nowhere."

But I couldn't stop. "Just a couple more, Aunty. Please!" After taking pictures from every angle, with a flash and without, I was finally satisfied. Rohit had barely touched the food while I had been clicking away.

"Aren't you eating?" I asked.

"I'm kinda full," he said. "You eat."

I forced him to eat a couple more bites, and finished the rest. I was exhausted from the emotional roller coaster I'd been on since this day began: from the anger at the fight on Canyon Hill, the shame of being caught eavesdropping, the panic at the fire and being chased by Psycho, and finally to the relief at being rescued by Shakuntala. Rohit was unusually quiet. I knew this old woman, sharing her home and meager meal with us, had touched him, too. And he was probably still worried to death about his parents.

When we'd finished eating, Shakuntala gathered the plates and put them outside. "The rain will clean them up and I'll have less washing tomorrow," she said. Her lips flapped over her gums, making it a little difficult to understand what she was saying.

"Rest now. It will be dawn in a few hours and I'll walk you to the scootie stand."

"Thank you for sharing your food with us," I said, trying not to sound too choked up and wimpy. "But how is it that you're living alone . . . at this age? Do you have kids? A husband?"

"My husband passed away many years ago. I have two sons. They are both living in the house I bought with my pension from teaching," she said without a trace of bitterness in her voice.

Rohit asked the question that was on the tip of my tongue. "So, why can't you live with them?"

"There's no room for me," she said softly. "I signed my property over to them, trusting they would look after me in my old age. But they did not." She stroked Moti's head, then stopped, deep in thought. Moti butted her hand gently with his nose and she resumed the calming ritual while he sighed deeply and closed his eyes.

"Aren't you mad at them?" I said, angry at the way she lived, wondering how her kids could be so mean.

"I forgave them a long time ago," said the old woman with a shrug. "As I said before, it's the one thing in life that is in our control. The rest is up to God. I'm very tired and so is Moti. Goodnight."

Rohit and I lay down where we sat while Moti and Shakuntala snuggled up on the thin reed mat, their noses touching on the tattered pillow.

Within moments she was snoring. It drowned out the clicking of my camera as I took a dozen more pictures, her words ringing in my head.

I forgave them a long time ago. It's the one thing in life that is in our control.

TWENTY

THE POUNDING OF THE RAIN OUTSIDE HAD TURNED to a light patter. I couldn't sleep.

"Ro?" I whispered.

"Yeah?"

"Thanks for saving me from the fire," I said.

"You saved me later," he replied. "We're even."

"But are we cool? Are you still mad at me?"

"A little," he said.

I sat up. He did, too. The air smelled of wet earth, and the steady drip of water in the pots and pans was calming. We sat next to each other, leaning against the wall.

"I'm sorry I didn't tell your mom I wanted to go back to New York," I said. "The fact is, I *didn't* want to go. Not so soon."

"Why?"

"Mom and Dad are going on a trial separation. They'll probably get a divorce before the year is over."

Silence. A loud snore from Shakuntala. A tinier one from Moti. And the drip-drip of water around us.

The kerosene lamp was out but his hand found my arm in the darkness and squeezed it reassuringly. "Why didn't you tell me?"

"Because I wasn't ready to say it out loud."

"That's stupid," he said.

"I wanted to have a vacation with my second family before I went back," I said. "In the last couple of years things have been going from bad to worse. Did you never wonder why I came over to your place more than I invited you over to mine? And it was always when my parents were away."

Rohit took a deep breath. "Yeah, but who cared as long as we were together and had fun?"

"That's because they fight every time they're in a room together. Dad's expectations of his family have been growing along with his business. He wants everything to be perfect—especially me." Now that the dam had cracked, there was no stopping me. I didn't even care if Shakuntala and Moti heard. The hurt and anger had been like poison in my blood and I wanted it out.

"You're doing well at school," said Rohit. "What else does he want?"

"He wants to be proud of me, of my achievements, so he can brag in front of his club buddies. According to him, the things I love—photography and food—are a waste of time. He blames Mom for the way I've turned out. They've had so many fights about it, I'm sure *I'm* the reason they're splitting."

Rohit moved closer, sliding his arm around my shoulder. "I

think you're a supercool friend, most times. *I'm* proud of you. And I think you're wrong. If they're splitting, it's not your fault!"

"Thanks," I said and meant it. "Dad wants me to drop photography and take up soccer next year. Just thinking about it makes me want to barf. I told him I hated soccer and I'd never join. Photography's my thing. At least for now. He got really upset with me. With Mom, too, for always taking my side."

Rohit sat back and looked at me, the dim streetlight reflecting off his glasses. "So, *now* I get the competition thing. That's why you want to win so badly."

"Yeah," I said, trying to control the wobble in my voice. "It's a chance to prove I'm good at *something*. It may not be enough to save my family but it'll be one thing less they fight about."

"Life's not fair," said Rohit. "But if it's any help, I'm in the same boat."

"Being a kid sucks!" I said.

"Being an orphan would suck even more. Earlier, I *hated* Ma and Papa. I wished they would go away and leave me alone, and now my wish might come—" He stopped abruptly. "I'll have no choice but to live with Bua," he finished in a choked voice.

It was my turn to reassure him. "They're fine," I said. "I know it. You're really lucky. Your mom can get a bit bossy at times, but at least she cares. Even your dad."

"And you think your parents don't care?" he said.

"Probably not." All those lonely evenings at home flashed

through my mind. "They're so busy with their lives, sometimes they forget about me."

Though it was murky inside the hovel, I could feel his eyes boring into me. "You're wrong."

"So now you know my parents better than I do?" I said, trying not to snap at him.

"What I do know is that Ma calls your parents every couple of days to let them know you're okay," he said. "Did you know that?"

"No, I—you serious?" I asked, not daring to believe him, yet wanting to with all my heart.

"I overheard Ma talking to your mom late one night when we were in Mumbai," said Rohit. "I only found out because I got up to use the bathroom. I think it's because you refused to carry a cell phone and your emails have been super brief. I was going to tell you, but then I was mad at you and forgot."

I felt like a jerk for thinking Mom and Dad didn't care. As soon as we got back to the flat, I was calling home for sure.

"Thanks for telling me," I said.

"You believe me, right?" he replied.

"Yeah, I do."

"Good," he replied. "Because I'm not punking you this time."

"I know. And there's no way I'm letting you get left behind in India. Even if it means I have to lock Boa up somewhere and throw away the key till our plane takes off."

He punched me. I punched him back and grabbed him before he toppled over and woke our hosts.

TWENTY-ONE

I HADN'T EXPECTED TO FALL ASLEEP AFTER ALL THE heavy stuff Ro and I talked about, but I did. I woke up to someone scrubbing my face with a rough, wet, disgustingly smelly rag.

"Arghhh, stop that," I said, opening my eyes.

Moti eyeballed me, his face inches away from mine, his tail wagging like crazy. I pushed him away and sat up. Pale light was streaming in through the grimy window covered with layers of plastic. Shakuntala was sipping a cup of tea. The smell of milk and ginger filled the tiny hovel. In the light of day, the place looked especially dismal and cheerless.

"Good morning," she said, smiling.

"Morning, Aunty," I said. "What time is it?"

"I don't have a clock or watch but I would guess about six thirty."

"Ro, wake up!" I said, shaking him gently. "Time to go."

He was up instantly, rubbing his eyes with his knuckles. "Ready."

"Would you like a cup of tea before you leave?" Shakuntala asked. "But I will understand if you want to go right away."

"We'd like to go now," we said in unison. I could only imagine the state Mrs. Lal would be in with her only son and his friend missing. I hoped they were all right.

Shakuntala put her cracked teacup down and covered it with a chipped plate. Then she picked up a staff from the side of the door and shuffled out, Moti at her heels. We followed close behind. Lolly-land looked clean and fresh after last night's rain. Even the green looked . . . greener.

"Hang on!" I said. "Forgot my camera." I dived back in and grabbed the camera I had deliberately left behind. I hurriedly pulled out all the money I had in my pockets—3,017 rupees and some change. I put all of it on top of the plate that covered Shakuntala's tea. I knew she wouldn't accept money from me, but at least this way she might be able to buy food for a few days. I took one last look at this hovel that had brought Ro and me together again before slipping out the door. It was amazing how such a tiny shack could be filled with more love than my entire brownstone.

• • • • • •

Shakuntala set off down the road at a slow yet steady pace. I kept an eye out for Rafiq, but like the night shadows, he had melted away in the crisp light of dawn.

We'd barely taken a few steps along the road when a

scootie screeched to a halt behind us. I leaped almost a foot in the air as visions of Rafiq chasing us down flitted through my head.

The Lals and Muscles, aka Khan, the driver we'd met when we arrived in Lolly-land, spilled out. Rohit's parents were red-eyed and bedraggled, soot marks from last night's fire still staining their faces and clothes. It was clear that they hadn't gone back to the flat, even to change.

Mrs. Lal launched herself at us, crying and laughing at the same time. "Rohit! Dylan!" she said. "Thank God you both are all right. I don't know what I would have done if . . ."

Rohit hugged her tight and then grabbed his dad, his face scrunched up. I knew he was trying hard not to bawl. Mrs. Lal hugged me, too, and the lump in my throat made it nearly impossible to speak. "Shakuntala here was nice enough to take us in when we got lost."

"Thank you, Shakuntala," said Mrs. L. "We are in your debt."

"Don't mention it," Shakuntala replied, smiling, her pink gums on full display.

"Did you shatter your glasses while running from the theater?" asked Mrs. Lal.

Rohit nodded.

"Good thing I packed the spare with me," said Mrs. Lal. "They're at the flat."

Khan and Shakuntala exchanged a few words while the rest of us did a group hug again and again.

"We asked every paramedic and passerby if they'd seen a *gora* with an Indian boy. Sorry, Dylan," she said, noticing my expression. "You do stand out, and it was the easiest way to describe you two."

"Uh-huh," I said.

"Anyway, an old man in tattered clothes and a floppy hat said he saw you both being put into an ambulance." Her voice shook and she gulped. "We raced to the hospital."

Rohit and I exchanged a look. It had to be Rafiq. He must have misled them so he could follow us.

"When we found that you weren't at the hospital, we raced back here and circled the theater, calling out for you. That's when Khan saw us and offered to take us around in the scootie. We've been to the hospitals and police stations in Deolali and Nashik, and everywhere in between. Why did you boys leave the area? And, Rohit, why didn't you answer your cell phone? I called about a thousand times!"

Rohit cleared his throat and I knew he was in for the scolding of his life. In front of an audience. He had already been through too much. I couldn't stand by and do nothing.

"Er, Mrs. Lal, it's *my* fault," I piped in just as Ro opened his mouth. "I asked Rohit to lend me his phone and then . . . I forgot to return it. It's still at the flat. I'm very, very sorry, Mrs. L!"

Rohit's jaw dropped, and Mrs. Lal's face turned red as she tried to contain her anger. I knew she wouldn't yell at me as much as she would at her own son.

"That was *very* careless of you, Dylan," she said in a stern voice. "You too, Rohit. One call could have saved us hours of worry. Do you know that even to file a missing person's report we have to wait twenty-four hours? The police could not help. So thoughtless . . . My heart almost stopped when I couldn't reach you . . ." Her voice trailed off as she shook her head and sniffed hard.

"Sorry, Ma." Ro's grateful eyes met mine.

"Sorry, Mrs. L," I said, and really meant it.

"I had to call your parents, Dylan," said Mrs. Lal. "They're out of their minds with worry. We have to call them right away to let them know you're safe."

I felt strangely elated and terrible hearing that. "Sure."

"I still don't understand why you boys didn't think of calling us from a public—"

"That's enough, Priya," Mr. Lal said, gently but firmly. "The important thing is that the boys are safe. Let's go home. We could all do with breakfast, a shower, and some sleep."

"You're right, Arun," said Mrs. Lal, her voice shaky. "But last night proved to me that family is everything, and without it money means nothing. We'll sell the Deolali flat immediately and use the money to get us through the next few months. I'll get a job as soon as we go back. But after today we're not taking a cent from your sister and she's *never* going to dictate terms to me or my family ever again. In fact, I've decided that we should leave as soon as the wedding is over."

Mr. Lal opened his mouth to speak but Mrs. Lal held up her hand, silencing him. "This is not open to discussion, Arun. My decision is final."

My faith in Mrs. Lal was justified. When this lady went to battle, she won. Always.

And that was that. Rohit and I exchanged excited grins. The horrible night hadn't turned out so badly after all. His parents were alive, I had my best friend back, and I'd taken some amazing pictures, too. There was just one thing left to do and that was to call Mom and Dad. I wasn't even upset that we were heading home earlier!

Shakuntala had been standing to the side quietly observing the entire exchange between the Lals and me. I hugged her goodbye and thanked her. "I'd like to mail you copies of the pictures I took," I said. "Will you please give me your address?"

"The municipal authorities are planning to tear down the huts by the end of the year. I won't have an address. You are a kind boy but I already have a picture of you, here." She touched her heart. "And why would I need a picture of Moti when I have the real thing?" Then she kissed my forehead (I had to stoop for it), and Rohit's, too. With Moti at her side, she walked away.

I took one last picture. Not for the competition but for me.

TWENTY-TWO

"**M**OM! IT'S ME," I SAID.

"Dylan!" Mom's panicked voice burst into my ear. "Thank God you're all right. We've been out of our minds with worry. Your dad and I booked tickets to come to Mumbai. We leave tonight, New York time."

I was so choked up I could barely speak. I turned away from the Lals, who stood outside the telephone booth watching me, and slyly wiped my eyes.

"Mom, cancel your tickets. I'm okay. Really!" I said, as calmly as I could manage. "We were lost after we got separated from Rohit's parents. An old lady gave us shelter from the rain. We all met up in the morning and everyone's good." I omitted mentioning Rafiq, sure she'd grab her purse and head to the airport *now* if I told her. "How are you and Dad doing?"

"Here, he wants to talk to you," she said.

There was muffled conversation in the background and then Dad came on the line.

"Son, you okay?" His voice was shaky. "I was so worried."

"I'm fine, Dad. I know you're busy so please cancel your tickets. I'll be home in a few days, anyway."

Silence.

"Dad?"

"Yeah. I . . . I just wanted to say that you're more important than any contract. And if you need us, we'll be there."

That was a first from him and it felt good. It was almost worth the horrible night just to hear him say that. "Thanks, Dad, but really, there's no need. I'm safe. We're heading back to Mumbai tomorrow. The wedding's the day after and then we're all leaving early for home. The Lals have some urgent work to take care of in New York."

"Great, son. I'll take the day off and pick you up at the airport," he said. "We'll spend it together as a family. We haven't done that in a long time."

Another first that I was going to hold him to. "Thanks, Dad. I'd like that. I got some great pictures I'd love to show you. I'm sure one of them will win something in the *National Geographic* competition I'm entering."

Silence.

"And, Dad?" I said, gathering the courage to go on.

"Yes, I heard you."

"I'm not signing up for soccer when I get back, whether I win something or not."

"Can we discuss it when you get here?"

"Sure," I said. This time I wasn't upset or even angry. I'd seen Mrs. Lal stand up to Mr. Lal about Boa, and Shakuntala survive her family's betrayal and a harsh life with only a dog as her friend. They'd been brave when things were tough and I guess I felt inspired and encouraged by them. I was going to convince Dad to see my side of things and I was going to stand my ground no matter what. "All I'll say is that you've made the choice to do something you're good at and that makes you happy, and I want that same choice."

There was a long silence and I wondered if we'd end up arguing again. "Fair enough," said Dad, surprising me.

"Thanks. Um . . . can I talk to Mom, please?"

"Rosemary?" Dad said. "Here."

Mom came back on the line. "You sure you're okay?"

"Yes, Mom, I'm fine. Just promise me you and Dad won't make any decisions about our family till I get back. You know . . . I mean—"

"I know what you mean, Dylan," she cut in. Mom was quiet for a minute before she spoke. "I can't promise anything but we'll have a discussion, all three of us, when you get back. I think it's long overdue."

I could live with that. "Sounds good."

The numbers in red, displaying the cost of the call, climbed rapidly and I was sure Mrs. Lal would insist on paying. I had to end the call soon if I didn't want her to pay a small fortune.

"Have to go, Mom," I said. "Love you."

"Love you, too," she said softly. "Don't you ever doubt that."

Smiling, I put down the phone. If she and Dad were going to try at making our family work, so would I. Shakuntala's words came back to me: *Just forgive and forget. Sometimes it's the only thing in your control.*

TWENTY-THREE

VT STATION WAS EVEN MORE PACKED WHEN WE got to Mumbai, as if the population had multiplied exponentially while we'd been away.

We were sucked into a whirlpool of sweaty humanity as soon as we stepped off the train. I stayed close to Rohit as a *fat* porter (the only one I'd seen in India) grabbed all our luggage in one go, waddled out of the station, and put us in the taxi line. Sweat dripped off his beet-red face but he somehow moved with ease.

As we stood on the curb waiting, a guy with bright-red lips sauntered past. He was chewing something and as I watched he spat straight onto the road. I jumped back as something that looked like red vomit hit the grate at our feet and splattered the sidewalk. It looked exactly like blood. I slowly turned to Ro.

"You liar! *That's* the bloodshed you've seen?" I said, elbowing him hard in the ribs.

Rohit smiled. "I promised you'd see it before you left Mumbai, and I kept my word."

"Chewing *paan* in public should be banned," Mrs. Lal said, her face screwed up in disgust. "And all these people should be made to scrub the walls and streets as punishment."

Now that I knew what the red stains really were, I noticed them everywhere. That was a lot of spit. Gross! New York didn't seem quite so bad now.

We reached the front of the cab line and piled into a waiting taxi.

"I wonder how the wedding preparations are coming on," Mr. Lal said calmly as the cabdriver narrowly missed mowing down a cyclist.

"Watch out!" I yelled from the backseat.

"*Gora baba*, shut mouth please," the driver said, glaring at me through the rearview mirror. "Every day, I do this."

I wondered if he meant he avoided decapitating a cyclist or drove like a blindfolded maniac every day. I stayed quiet but squinched my eyes closed as we hurtled through the narrow streets of Mumbai toward the Lals' flat.

"Nisha's parents are very well organized," said Mrs. Lal. "I'm sure the preparations will be superb in spite of the monsoons. It'll be good to attend a wedding in the family after so long."

"Can't wait for the biryani and *mithai*," said Mr. Lal. "Tasty food at last."

"You mean mine isn't?" said Mrs. Lal in mock anger.

Mr. Lal backtracked immediately. "No one could beat your

food, my *dear*. I only meant in the time since you were gone. I've been eating out and the food was terrible."

Placated, Mrs. Lal nodded. Mr. Lal was one smart dude. Most times. How would Boa react to Mrs. Lal's decision about Rohit and the knowledge that her days of bullying the Lals were over? *That* would make an awesome Bollywood scene.

· • · • · •

The phone was ringing when we entered the flat, its tinny sound echoing in the stuffy room. Mr. Lal raced to answer it while Mrs. Lal surveyed the contents of the fridge.

I stepped into the bathroom and eyed the toilet with deep affection. Lolly-land had been an exciting adventure but crouching over an Indian-style toilet was like trying to keep your balance over a gaping hole and trying to *go* while someone squeezed you tightly around the waist. Peeing was hard, too, because I always ended up in the splash zone. I've never thought so much about using the bathroom before!

Note to Self: Value the ordinary. Especially the Western crapper.

"I've ordered food from a restaurant," said Mrs. Lal as I emerged from the bathroom. "You boys have lunch and relax. All the activity starts again tomorrow."

"Won't you be eating with us?" asked Rohit.

"No, we're going to meet Bua first and then a few others," said Mrs. Lal, her voice firm, eyes steely. "We'll be back late at night. It won't be fun for either of you so stay here and chill."

"Cool, Mrs. L," I said, glad Rohit and I wouldn't be anywhere in the vicinity when Boa got the news.

"Thanks, Ma," Rohit said. "Bua's going to be really mad. You sure you don't need backup? Dylan and I can go with you."

Mrs. Lal shook her head. "It's best if you weren't there but thanks, *Beta*. This is our family and we decide what happens to it. If she doesn't like it, that's too bad. We're better off getting this unpleasantness out of the way before the wedding."

"We'll need to be a bit subtle, Priya," said Mr. Lal, looking thoroughly uncomfortable. "After all, she only wants the best for us. It's not as if she's trying to boss us around."

"Yes, she is," snapped Mrs. Lal. "You weren't there at the reception but that is exactly what she tried."

Mr. Lal looked skeptical. I knew it was the right time for the video I'd taken of Boa threatening Mrs. L at the engagement party.

"If it's any help, I'd like to show you both something," I said.

The Lals looked at me in surprise. I grabbed my camera, scrolled through the archives, and pressed play. They watched in complete silence and then it was Mr. Lal's turn to look grim.

"I had no idea," he said, sitting down heavily on a chair. "*I had no idea at all*. You leave her to me, Priya. It's time I showed her who runs my family."

Mrs. Lal threw me a grateful look and Rohit thumped me on the back. Who said photography didn't pay? My camera had just helped save a family.

There was a knock on the door. I went over and opened it. A boy stood on the landing with two plastic bags. "Four hundred rupees, please," he said politely.

Mr. Lal paid him while Rohit and I laid out the food on the table. There was saffron rice, chicken curry swimming in a golden-orange pool of oil, cauliflower with potatoes and peas sprinkled liberally with cilantro, and hot *naans*, glistening with butter. My mouth watered.

I ladled hot rice and chicken curry onto my plate, then added a handful of raw onions and a generous squeeze of lemon juice all over it. My time with the Lals had taught me that this was the best way to eat curry and rice. The fresh lemon juice added just the right amount of tang and the onions gave it a bit of kick to jazz it up. I was really going to miss eating like this every day.

The phone rang again. Mr. Lal picked it up. "Yes, we just got in from Deolali. Priya is getting dressed and then we'll be right over. I know, I know. Lots of people to see."

Mr. and Mrs. Lal quickly got ready and hurried off to meet the clan, starting with the snake. Outside, the sky was almost black with rain clouds. Ominous rumbles echoed through the sticky air.

I downloaded all my pictures onto my laptop. The one with

Shakuntala and Moti eating from the same plate was perfect. The lighting (I'd used a soft filter for that one), the composition, even the clarity had turned out exactly the way I'd wanted. Just looking at it gave me goose bumps. Another good one was of the time when they'd been asleep, noses touching. But I also really liked the last one I'd taken as they'd walked away. An old lady and her dog, a strange and sweet friendship that didn't require words.

"I love these," said Rohit. "You're definitely going to win *something* if not first prize!"

I'd been so lost in the images, I hadn't noticed he'd pulled up a chair next to me and was peering at the screen intently. "You think so?"

"I know so!" he said. "I lied when I said earlier that you weren't good. Sorry."

"Forget it."

We sipped hot chocolate as the monsoons unleashed their annual fury on Mumbai. Huddled at the dining table, we discussed the pictures some more and finally agreed that the one with Shakuntala and Moti eating off of one plate best captured the friendship theme. I uploaded the picture to the *National Geographic* website.

Though I really wanted to win, I knew it wouldn't be the end of the world if I didn't. Ro and I were friends again. Even though it had taken a scary situation, I knew my parents cared about me. And on top of it all, I knew I was going to be able to stand up to Dad when we got back. After Boa, the near-death experience with the fire, and being chased by Rafiq, handling a stubborn dad didn't seem that hard.

I looked out the window. The rain had let up and the sun shone from behind the thunderclouds, outlining them in gold.

TWENTY-FOUR

THE NEXT MORNING I WOKE UP TO THE SOUND OF heavy rain and the scent of tea and *aloo parathas*. What a swag way to wake up—and way more effective than an alarm clock. If only I could patent *paratha*-flavored instant oatmeal in the States, I'd be rich and famous.

I hurried to the window. The narrow lane looked dismal through a curtain of rain. The road was submerged in at least two feet of water. Plastic bags, bottles, banana peels, and other unidentifiable debris floated on the floodwater's pockmarked surface. Everything was soggy and limp in the relentless downpour.

"OMG!" I said, aghast. "We'll need a boat to get through this."

Rohit joined me at the window, yawning. "Close, but not yet. Give it a couple more hours."

"Do we have enough food if we get rained in?" I asked, staring at the blurry world beyond the window. "Do people actually go out in these conditions?"

Rohit laughed and slipped an arm around my shoulders.

"Looks like I might win my bet after all . . . that is, if you survive this mess."

I was about to object when I saw his glinting eyes and his grin. "Keep your money ready, Ro. You'll be handing it over soon."

"Boys, breakfast!" Mrs. Lal called out.

We were at the table in under a minute. I sipped hot chocolate and munched on *aloo parathas* smothered in ghee. The taste was pure heaven. I finished my second *paratha* and sat back stuffed and in a very good mood.

"How did Bua take the news that I wasn't staying?" asked Rohit.

Mr. Lal's expression turned stony; Mrs. Lal smiled. "Not well," she said. "Bua refused to believe I was serious. She'll definitely try and corner you at the wedding today, Rohit. Just be polite and tell her to talk to me. Better yet, try and avoid her altogether."

"Papa, she's your sister. Why don't you tell her to leave us alone?"

He shrugged. "She likes to be in control. She hates it that I am actually refusing to do as she asks. I don't think it's sunk in completely yet."

Rohit and I exchanged glances. So, this wasn't over. Not till we were on the plane to New York would Ro be safe.

"Too bad," Mrs. Lal said. "You're no longer a kid, Arun, and you have to live life on your own terms."

"I did tell her, didn't I?" said Mr. Lal. "Can we just drop this now?"

"WTF," said Mrs. L. "Right, guys?"

"*Ma!*"

"Mrs. L?"

"*Priya?*"

"What?" she said, looking at our shocked expressions.

"I can't believe you would swear at me in front of the kids," said Mr. Lal, looking really hurt.

"All I said was 'Well That's Fine.' How's that swearing?"

"Ma, that's not what WTF stands for," said Rohit. He whispered the correct meaning to her and I watched her face turn red. "Stick with the full forms, okay, Ma?"

"Okay," she replied. "Sorry, Arun. Boys. I think abbreviations are most confusing and should be banned."

"How are we going to get to the banquet hall for the wedding?" I asked, staring out the window. "This is not looking good."

"We'll manage," said Mrs. Lal.

But apparently the hundreds of other wedding guests were worried about it, too. The phone rang nonstop as plans were made and remade. Yes, the wedding was still on. Would someone be able to send a car for us? Not likely. Most of the roads in Mumbai were flooded. A few buses were running in the suburbs, where the flooding wasn't *too* bad, but everything was stalled in the downtown area.

Finally when there was a lull in the calls, Mr. Lal stood up. "The *Baraat* arrives at the hotel at noon. It's already ten. We better start moving."

"But how?" asked Rohit, who'd stuck his head out the window and was trying to get a glimpse of the main road beyond the lane. "I don't see any cars moving."

"We'll walk to the main road and cross the bridge to Marine Drive. From there we'll have a better chance of getting a cab to take us to the hotel," said Mr. Lal calmly. "Worst-case scenario, we'll walk to Oberoi Towers. It shouldn't take us more than an hour."

"Walk?" I spluttered. "It's a swimming pool out there!"

"Now do you see why I tried to force you to take professional swimming lessons with me? This isn't the same as swimming in your pool," Rohit said and winked. He saw my face and came over to pat me on the back. "Don't worry, we'll all help you stay on your feet. Just keep your mouth shut so you don't swallow a rat . . . or something worse."

My stomach suddenly felt queasy and the second *paratha* I'd eaten climbed up my throat, threatening to make a reappearance. I was glad I hadn't gone in for a third.

"Don't scare him, Rohit," said Mrs. Lal. "It won't be so bad, Dylan. The water will not be higher than your waist yet. You'll be able to walk quite easily as long as you follow our instructions."

"And our clothes?" I asked. "We'll get there soaking wet."

"Who said we're wearing clothes?" said Rohit.

"What?" I squeaked, as visions of wading to the hotel in my birthday suit flashed through my mind. Then I saw the upward curve of his mouth. He'd punked me again.

"Monsoon wedding organizers have it down to a science. There'll be changing rooms at the hotel. Though honestly, Ma, why can't I stay at home with Dylan and watch TV? He doesn't want to go, right, Dylan?"

I was torn. If I played it safe, I might never get another chance to see or photograph an Indian wedding. One thing Dad had drilled into me was to *always* open the door when opportunity knocked.

Then there was this crazy downpour, the fact that I swam like a drowning rat, and the realization that I might not be the *only* drowning rat in the water. All eyes were on me. I saw disappointment in Mrs. Lal's, amusement in Mr. Lal's, and pure mischief in Rohit's. I made up my mind.

"Let's go," I said. "I'm sure I'll manage with all of you helping me."

"Okay, everyone," said Mrs. Lal. "Gather your party clothes and shoes and put them on the table. I'll pack them in a plastic bag that you will carry on your head, *above* the water. Wear shorts, T-shirts, and flip-flops. Nothing fancy," she said, looking straight at me.

I got the distinct impression we were embarking on a dangerous mission; man against nature. Only time would tell whether we, or the floods, would win.

Within fifteen minutes we were ready. All our clothes were double wrapped in plastic bags. The Lals had gifted me a cream-colored silk kurta-pajama to wear at the wedding and I had no plans to let the water ruin it. I'd also wrapped my camera in three layers of plastic and hung it around my neck. Even though I didn't need any more pictures for the competition, I didn't want to leave it behind. There would be lots of photo ops for my portfolio and I didn't want to miss any.

"Hold it, Dylan," said Mr. Lal just as we reached the door. I stopped.

"You can't wear those," he said, pointing at my Nikes. "They'll be soaked as soon as you step outside. Wear a pair of Rohit's rubber flip-flops."

I stripped off my socks and shoes, and stuck my feet into the flip-flops Rohit gave me. The rubber part between my big and middle toes felt weird. At every step, the flip-flops slapped my soles, threatening to fall off. But it was that or ruin my expensive shoes. I squared my shoulders and nodded.

"Ready?" asked Mrs. Lal, her eyes steely.

"Ready," we replied in chorus, then picked up our respective parcels and trooped downstairs.

"Okay, people," said Mr. Lal. "We're going in."

· • · · • ·

Water flooded the building's foyer and lapped against the bottom two stairs. More debris floated past lazily and collected in the corners. A horrible stench hit my nose and I took a shallow breath, trying to keep my breakfast down. I'd wanted to see the *real* Mumbai and now here it was, right at my feet.

"Let's go," Mr. Lal said and stepped into the muck. Rohit's face was scrunched up, as if in pain. His elbows twitched as he threw me a quick glance. Then he stepped in. Mrs. Lal followed. Something furry floated by. I stood on the steps, frozen. This was beyond gross. I couldn't do it. I just *couldn't*.

"Come along, Dylan," said Mr. Lal. "We don't have all day while you study the water. Best not to think too much. Wade in."

From the corner of my eye I saw something brown surface, then dive back into the murky depths, creating a ripple. I took a deep breath and stepped in. The water was cold as it crept up my legs, all the way to my knees. We sloshed to the entrance and out into the lane. The water crawled up to my waist.

"Crap!" I said. "Can't we hire a boat from the marina?"

"We should have packed an inflatable raft," said Rohit, flicking his glasses up and looking around with a gloomy expression. He was wearing the spare pair his mother had carried, and they seemed even looser than his previous pair that had shattered.

"Excellent idea," I said, trying not to shriek as something brushed past my ankle.

"Enough with the commentary," said Mr. Lal. "Move."

He took the lead and we waded to the end of the lane and out onto the main road. We passed kids splashing around in the water. Adults shuffled past with parcels tied on top of their heads, leaving their hands free. They walked confidently as if this was normal. Which I guess it probably was during the monsoon season. This would have been an *awesome* photo op, but I was so worried about ruining my camera; I couldn't risk unwrapping the plastic around it. And it was tough keeping my balance with a bundle of clothes perched on my head and flip-flops threatening to drift away at every step. The rain came down hard and within seconds I was drenched from head to toe. Mrs. Lal had told me not to bother with an umbrella or even a rain jacket. That stuff was made for civilized rainfall. Not the savage fury that pummeled Mumbai for three months every year.

"Ughh! Something touched me!" I yelped.

"Keep walking," said Rohit. "And don't look at the water. It'll only slow you down."

Cars parked along the sides were submerged up to their door handles. More debris floated our way. I tried not to think about what it could be. *Mind over matter. Focus on the goal.* Though, now that I was here, I *really* wished I'd stayed home. I would rather have starved than wade through garbage water.

"Keep to the center of the road at all times," said Mr. Lal. "Follow me and *do not stray to the side.*"

It reminded me of Gollum's warning to Frodo and Sam as they took the shortcut across the Dead Marshes to Mount Doom. *Don't follow the lights,* Gollum had said. If I weren't feeling so miserable and cold, I would have laughed.

"Why?" I asked. "What about the traffic?"

"There won't be any traffic today," Mr. Lal said. "Forget cars, not even a *truck* could get through the side roads today. You're safe if you stay in the middle."

And he was right. Lots of people moved past us, keeping to the center of the road. I had to admire their tenacity. No matter what the weather—scorching heat or massive downpour—nothing fazed them. As I struggled on, I realized just how lucky I was to be living in America. I took so much for granted. One thing I was sure of: If I made it out of this downpour alive, I'd whine less about things, especially the weather.

The bloated body of a dead cat suddenly popped up in front of me. I yelped and swerved.

"DYLAN, watch out!" yelled Rohit.

Too late. I lost my balance and plunged into the filthy, murky water. I flailed around and opened my mouth. *Big Mistake*. A plastic bag sailed in. I gagged, throwing up and swallowing at the same time. Blackness clouded my vision. This was it. The End. Goodbye, Mom, Dad, Ro. I love you all.

Suddenly there was light and I could breathe again. I drew in a lungful of air, shuddering and shivering, wiping water from my eyes, blinking hard. Rohit still held a fistful of my T-shirt as he stared into my face. In his other hand was my parcel of clothes as well as his own.

"Dylan, are you all right?" Mrs. Lal shrieked. "Speak to me!" Her face was as gray as the water around us.

Rohit let go of my shirt but stayed close. "Are you okay?"

"I'm . . . okay," I managed to gasp. "Lost my balance, that's all."

"Good thing you were in the middle of the road," said Mr. Lal, his voice grim. "There are uncovered manholes along the sides. Idiots from the local municipality open them for repairs and forget about them. The rains come and they're hidden. Many people, especially kids, have died because they got sucked into the manholes. Once they're in, there's no getting them out till it's too late."

I felt like throwing up again. What if I'd been at the side and Rohit hadn't pulled me out in time? By now my ghost would be exploring Mumbai's sewer system. How had this weakling managed to hang on to someone three times his weight? I hugged him tight, not caring about the strange looks I was getting from passersby.

"Are you okay to go on?" asked Mrs. Lal in a shaky voice. "Or should we go home? I am *so* sorry you had to go through this, *Beta*. The monsoons can be pretty rough for someone experiencing them for the first time."

My heart still beat erratically in my chest and I wanted to sob. I looked at the expectant faces around me, waiting for a decision that would ruin this day or make it a memorable one. They'd traveled thousands of miles for this wedding. But they were willing to forego it for me.

I'd gotten so used to taking care of myself back home that at first my decision came quickly. We should go back to the flat and forget this suicide mission. But I couldn't. I forced myself to smile. "Did Frodo and Sam give up when the journey became dangerous? Did Harry Potter, when he was lost and alone in the Forbidden Forest? Onward, I say!"

The bedraggled Lal family smiled as one, their hair plastered to their heads and faces streaming with rain. *I loved them* and could not have asked for a better fellowship on my mission to Mumbai.

"You're a very brave boy, Dylan, and a thoughtful one, too," said Mrs. Lal. She patted my cheek. "My Rohit is lucky to have you as a friend."

"I think it's the other way around, Mrs. L," I said as cheerily as I could even though I still felt sick to my stomach and really wanted to wash out my mouth with Lysol. "But please don't tell Mom about this um . . . mishap. I'll tell her myself when we're home."

Mrs. Lal nodded and I could see she was relieved. Rohit linked his elbow with mine. "You're staying with me every step of the way, bro. You're *banned* from walking these streets alone during the rest of our stay."

I nodded, the warmth of his arm in mine giving me the courage to start walking again. It didn't even matter that I'd basically been banned from more activities in these two weeks than I had in my entire life back in New York.

TWENTY-FIVE

WE REACHED MARINE DRIVE WITHOUT ANOTHER near-death incident. The flooding wasn't so bad here and only a foot of water covered the road. Within ten minutes an empty cab crawled past. We stood in the middle of the road till the cabbie was forced to stop. We piled in, ignoring the driver's angry protests that the seats would be ruined.

"Oberoi Towers," said Mr. Lal. "*Jaldi karo* and I'll give you a generous tip."

The driver gave us a suspicious look through the rearview mirror. Tipping aside, we weren't decent enough to enter a McDonald's, let alone a five-star hotel. I really wanted a shower. There was no way I would let Nisha or any of the other guests see me this way.

As soon as our cab reached the hotel, Mr. Lal paid the driver, tipped him, and we all hurried to the door. It was already 11:45 and the groom's wedding procession was expected by noon. The doorman looked us over from head to toe. I'd lost a flip-flop when I'd fallen. Bits of dirt and hair were plastered to my bare legs.

"No beggars," he said coldly.

I stared at him, stunned. No one had ever turned me away like that or called me a beggar. Rohit's twitching started up and Mrs. Lal's face turned beet red. I looked down at my clothes and honestly couldn't blame the guy. *I* wouldn't let us into the hotel looking like we did.

"What rubbish," thundered Mr. Lal. "This"—he gestured to his clothes—"is because of that," he said, sweeping his hand at the rain.

The doorman looked at us in confusion.

"Do you know *who I am*?" Mr. Lal said, standing tall. Water dripped from his shorts and ran in rivulets down his scrawny, hairy legs and down to his flip-flop clad feet.

"Er . . . no," said the doorman. Though by his alarmed expression, he was probably thinking *lunatic*.

"I am Lal. I know the general manager of this hotel, his boss, even the local MP," Mr. Lal roared. "I will make sure you lose your job if you don't let us in. *Right now.*"

"Sorry, sir," said the doorman, looking thoroughly uncomfortable. "But you cannot go through the main lobby looking like that. Might I suggest the service entrance?"

People were stopping to stare at us. I felt like crap and was seriously thinking about diving behind the large potted plant at the entrance while Mr. Lal argued with the doorman. Mr. Lal sure was taking the man-mouse challenge issued by Mrs. Lal seriously; I'd never seen him this angry. Just then a car drew up. The rude man pushed us aside and rushed forward to open the door. Out stepped Nisha, wearing a gold-and-red saree, looking like a goddess. If a manhole were around, I would have jumped in voluntarily.

"What happened to you?" she asked in a soft voice. "My God, you all look like you've fought the *Mahabharata* just to get here."

"Something like that," I said, though I didn't have any clue what she was talking about. A gust of wind whistled through the covered walkway and I shivered.

"We couldn't get a cab so we had to walk partway," Mrs. Lal explained, trying to smooth her hair and wipe her face with a wet handkerchief.

Mr. Lal was still arguing with the doorman when Nisha's father emerged from the car, tucking his cell phone into his pocket. "Let them in, my good man," he said, pressing money into the doorman's palm. "They are all part of the wedding party, caught like chickens in the rain."

Without any other arguments, the doorman let us into the lobby. Now the air-conditioning chilled me to the bone. Luckily Nisha's father had booked a few extra rooms at the hotel for guests who wanted to shower and get dressed. We picked up key cards from reception and hurried upstairs. Mr. and Mrs. Lal took one room; Rohit and I took the other. I couldn't wait to wash off the street garbage clinging to every inch of me but I let Rohit go first. He'd earned it.

I stared out the window at the turbulent Arabian Sea crashing against the parapet. The tetrapods stood strong under pressure, just like my friendship with Ro.

· · · · · ·

Within fifteen minutes we were in the banquet hall, cleaned up and decked out in our silk outfits. We looked so good I insisted on taking selfies with Rohit and his parents.

"Let's go find the buffet," I said to Rohit. "You know, just to check on it, before things get started."

My senses were assaulted as we circled the banquet hall. The fragrances of perfume, incense, and food mingled in the air to create an overpowering smell. The sheer number of colors and patterns was dizzying. Sunglasses should probably be handed out at Indian weddings, just like they do with 3-D glasses at movie theaters back home.

I took a few pictures, wondering when it might be polite to start digging into the food. The walk to Marine Drive had made me hungrier than usual.

We saw Boa in the distance, in a bright-red saree, and immediately walked in the opposite direction. Neither of us wanted a run-in so soon, even though I knew at some point she was going to hunt Ro down and bully him.

"Dulha aa raha hai," a cry went up. *"Dulha aa raha hai!"*

"Translate," I said to Rohit as we followed the crowd to the large windows lining the banquet hall, overlooking the street.

"The groom's arriving," said Rohit. "You should find this interesting."

"Why?"

"Because he's not coming by car."

"You mean he's wading here in shorts, too? Cool, now I don't feel so bad."

Rohit pointed to the window. "Look."

There was Sanjay, on a tired white horse draped with a red-and-gold cloth that was bleeding color. The horse's butt and legs were tinged with red as if it were wounded. Bedraggled revelers danced behind Sanjay, trying to look cheerful despite the downpour. On either side was the band, wearing soaked red uniforms and hats fitted with mini umbrellas, playing Bollywood tunes while sloshing through ankle-deep water. They were so loud, I could hear them over the rain and through the thick glass windows.

Though an umbrella was attached to a weird contraption on the saddle, Sanjay was wet and looked super miserable while he tried to smile and wave at us. I almost felt like I was at the zoo, staring at an exotic animal.

"Poor guy," I said, clicking a couple of pictures. "Couldn't they have come by car just this once?"

"Tradition, dude, *tradition*. A little rain doesn't bother us," said Rohit, polishing his glasses for a better look. They slipped out of his hands and he stooped to retrieve them. "The groom *always* arrives on a horse," he said.

"And now, he's leaving," I said.

"What?" Rohit straightened up and jammed his glasses onto his nose.

The horse was galloping through the soaking wedding procession. The umbrella had fallen off and was now floating upside down in the water while Sanjay held on to the horse's mane for dear life. His relatives raced behind him, yelling for him to stop, but he wouldn't, or couldn't. I noticed something large and brown swinging at the end of the horse's tail but before I could get a better look, or zoom in to take a picture, they had disappeared around the corner.

"I can't believe it!" I said. "I wonder which movie *this* scene is from."

Rohit shook his head. "The question is, was it the horse who bolted or the groom?"

"Dulha bhag gaya!" someone yelled. *"Dulha bhag gaya!"*

The whisper traveled up and down the line of people peering out the window and echoed through the banquet hall. I didn't need a translation for that. The shocked whispers and horrified expressions were enough. The groom had run away. Poor Nisha.

"Wonder if he'll come back," someone remarked.

There were a few sniggers and rude laughs.

"What do you think made that horse bolt?" Rohit said. "I hope it wasn't *cold feet!*"

"Not funny," I said. "Did you see anything on the horse's tail? I'm sure I saw a drowning rat clinging to it."

"Probably poop," Rohit said, waving off my explanation.

"How do you think Nisha is going to feel when she hears this?" I said softly, still staring at the confusion on the street. The band stood there uncertainly, staring at one another, while relatives sloshed around in the water, shouting instructions. And still the rain came down. The relentless monsoons stopped for nothing. Not even tragedy and heartbreak.

"How dare he do that?" someone shrieked from the middle of the room. "How could he embarrass me like that?"

Nisha had just found out about her runaway groom. Everyone raced from the window toward the center of the banquet hall, where Nisha was having a meltdown. She yelled some more and then ran out of the hall, wailing. Sanjay had seemed like a nice guy, so why would he do something like this? The more I thought about it, the more I was convinced something else was going on.

"*Tch, tch*, another child with horrible manners," said a familiar voice behind us.

It felt as if I'd accidentally stuck my finger in an electrical socket. Rohit and I turned around slowly and there was Boa in her danger-red outfit and blood-red lips. Her eyes were gray pebbles. I almost expected her to sway menacingly like Kaa in *The Jungle Book*. *Trust in me . . . Shut your eyes and trust in me . . .*

"Hello, Bua," said Rohit in a strangled whisper.

"Think you can get away by letting your mother come to your rescue?" she hissed.

"He's *not* staying, Aunty," I said with false bravado. "You can't break up my friend's family. It's not right."

"I don't need a *gora* to tell me what's right and wrong. I cannot stand bad behavior and *you* are the reason I don't want him going back. Once he's here with me, you are *banned* from communicating with my nephew ever again! Do I make myself clear?"

My face burned. "How can you be so mean?" I snapped. "You poisonous snake!"

"I always get my way, *dear*," she said, pinching my cheek hard. "Always."

My eyes teared up. I raised my hand, ready to pinch her back.

"Gotta go," said Rohit as he took my arm and dragged me away. "Not worth it," he said to me.

"Not worth it?" I snapped. "She needs someone to teach her a lesson. She can't get away with being so horrible. Think of something, Rohit, or I will."

"For now, let's go see what's up with Nisha. She has bigger problems."

"You're right, bro. Let's see if we can go help."

TWENTY-SIX

WHISPERS ECHOED THROUGH THE CORRIDOR OUT-side the banquet hall. Nisha had locked herself in a bathroom stall and refused to come out. All the guests streamed toward said bathroom to witness the live drama.

"But . . . I think I know what happened . . ." I started to say, when I caught Rohit's eye. He was frowning and shaking his head.

"What?" I whispered to him.

"You'll make it worse by saying anything, especially since you're a foreigner. Just shut up and observe. It will work out in the end. Most Indian weddings have a bit of drama. This is part of the tradition, too."

A huge crowd had gathered outside the bathroom. Guests from other banquet halls who tried to use it were rudely turned away.

"What is the problem?" a woman asked, her eyes sparkling in anticipation of hearing some juicy bit of gossip.

"Emergency," was all she got. "Go use another one."

More came and were denied entry. They hobbled away in pain, searching for another bathroom along the super-long corridor. In the meantime, Nisha's family was trying to get her to go back to the banquet hall, promising that everything would be all right.

Anyone who could pull rank squeezed into the bathroom. Rohit and I managed to squirm our way in, too. We kept far away from Boa, who, as always, had bullied her way in. It was hot and stuffy and the air reeked of perfumes clashing with bathroom air freshener. But no one budged an inch.

"Nisha, come out now," her mother pleaded. "Your groom's not run away. There has to be a rational explanation and we will get to the bottom of this *as soon* as you come out. Please, my darling. Come out and I'll find you someone better than Sanjay. Today."

Silence.

"Nisha, this is your father. I *command* you to get out right now or I'll break the door down."

More silence.

A burly hotel security guard pushed his way in.

"Sir, this is a *ladies'* washroom, *gents* are not allowed in. Please leave now."

"Then what are *you* doing in here?" he bellowed. "My daughter's in there. I have to get her out and get her married. Go away and leave me alone."

"Brilliant logic in the face of pressure," I said, nudging Rohit.

He shushed me. The atmosphere was tense. Nisha's quiet sobbing was the only sound. I felt really sorry for her.

"But, sir, this is a *ladies'* room," the security guy persisted. "Let your wife talk to her."

"If you don't leave now," said Nisha's dad in a very quiet yet menacing voice, "I will stuff your head down the nearest toilet and then I will pull the flush. This is a matter of my family's honor and I'm not leaving. Get out!"

The security man retreated, muttering under his breath about crazy guests and how they were giving him ulcers, and how he wasn't paid enough for all the lunatics he had to deal with every day.

Nothing anyone said would get Nisha out.

"Go away," she wailed. "How could he humiliate me like this? It will be all over Facebook and Twitter by now. I'd rather die than show my face again."

Screams and gasps filled the bathroom. I couldn't stay quiet for a minute longer. As a photographer I prided myself in observing every little detail. I had to save this situation and speak up, *now*, no matter what. Sam hadn't hesitated to lay down his life for Frodo, nor Ron Weasley for Harry Potter, nor Grover for Percy Jackson. We saviors had no choice—we had to do what we had to do.

"A rat!" I yelled out over the din.

Thirty pairs of eyes swiveled in my direction. Nisha's father advanced, pushing aside the spectators. "Are you calling my son-in-law a rat, you ignorant boy?"

"Rohit . . . help . . ." I squeaked as Nisha's dad towered over me. "Don't let him kill me."

Rohit gulped. His hands twitched like crazy as he positioned himself between me and imminent death for the second time in one afternoon. "Uncle, my friend Dylan is a photographer."

I waved my camera under his nose.

"He has an excellent eye for detail," Rohit continued. "And what he is trying to say is he thinks he saw a rat on the horse's tail—"

"Shut up!" Nisha's mom said. "What do you know? Sanjay's family has always considered us beneath them. This was just a ploy to humiliate us. They must have found a bride who can give them more dowry."

Another agonized wail from the bathroom stall. "I hate him, I *hate* him. Please let me die in peace."

The crowd gasped as one. Someone fainted and had to be carried out. Another guest quickly snuck in to take her place.

"NISHA!" a familiar voice called out.

The crowd parted again as someone came rushing into the bathroom. This was the best Bollywood movie I'd watched since I'd landed in Mumbai and I was in it! If only I'd been able to record it all.

"Nisha, what are you doing in there? I refuse to get married in a bathroom stall. You better get out," said Sanjay. He was sopping wet, his turban askew, making a large puddle on the marble floor. He stank of salt water and seaweed.

"Get lost!" she screamed.

"I love you!" he yelled back, approaching the stall door. "If you're planning to die in this stall, I'll do the same in the next one. Or you could come out now and we could get married in the hall."

For a moment you could have heard a fly fart. Sanjay turned around to glare at all of us and went to pound on the door just as it flew open. His fist landed on Nisha's nose with a horrible crunch.

"Ahhhhh," she screamed as blood cascaded over her mouth and dripped from her chin onto her red-and-gold saree.

"You monster!" shrieked Nisha's mother.

"I'll break your bloody teeth!" roared her father. "Mistreating my darling child and you're not even married yet."

"Nisha," Sanjay said, ignoring them. "I'm so sorry. Are you okay?"

"Ogay," she said, dabbing her nose with a handful of toilet paper while her mother fussed over her. "Why did you run away?"

"I didn't. I think something spooked my horse. It bolted and dropped me into the water just around the corner. Thank God it wasn't on the tetrapods or in the sea! *I love you, Nisha* . . . How could you even think I'd run away?"

"Thank you," I said, taking a little bow.

Everyone ignored me.

Nisha wrapped her arms around him and everyone in the

room clapped. "Come on, let's get you cleaned up and then I'm going to marry you," Sanjay murmured. "I want to change out of these wet clothes as soon as possible."

The cheering crowd followed the bride and groom out of the bathroom. The disheveled band, which had regrouped outside, struck up a merry tune again and everyone headed back to the banquet hall.

Boa stayed behind till we were the only ones left. "As soon as you see your parents, send them to me," she said to Rohit before diving into the nearest stall.

Rohit stared at me in desperation. His twitch started up and I knew he was stressed all over again. Enough was enough with this bullying!

I looked around and saw a closet. Inside there was a maintenance sign along with a mop and janitor's bucket. I stared at it and then at Rohit. He caught on immediately. He grabbed the sign and the mop. I grabbed the bucket and we raced for the door. We switched off the lights and ducked out as Boa's screech filled the dark bathroom.

"Rohit Lal, you are the worst child I have ever met. And, Dylan, you are *forever banned from India*. I'll have you arrested if you ever set foot on Indian soil again. I know the police commissioner and the presi—"

We shut the bathroom door and jammed the mop and bucket against it so that the door could only be opened from the outside. Rohit put up the sign: UNDER MAINTENANCE. DO NOT ENTER.

Then we galloped away to the banquet hall, where the wet groom and bleeding bride sat before a gaunt priest wearing only a bedsheet wrapped around his waist. The priest was wringing his hands, muttering to himself. "The *shubh mahurat* is over. Now that the auspicious time for the wedding has passed, you cannot get married for ninety-seven years. Please pay me my dues and goodnight."

"Are you mad, Punditji?" asked Sanjay. "The *shubh mahurat* is when I say it is. Marry us right now."

And the wedding finally began, two hours late. Nisha and Sanjay were married without any other Bollywood moments. I was happy to have played a small part in it. Nisha came up to me later and kissed me on both cheeks. Even with a swollen nose, she looked beautiful.

"You are a wonderful boy, Dylan. I will always remember you and your timely help. Thank you."

· · · · · ·

Rohit and I stood side by side at the glass windows overlooking the Arabian Sea. He handed me a piece of paper. It read: IOU $100.

"Since we're leaving early, you won the bet," Rohit said with a smile.

I tore up the paper and shoved the bits into my pocket. "Couldn't have done it without you, bro. This was the *best* vacation of my life!"

Rohit was quiet for a moment. He twitched, shoved his glasses up his nose, and then said, "Ditto, but only because you were with me."

He punched me. I punched back, lightly. Then I turned to face the sea of people in the banquet hall, eating, laughing, and enjoying themselves.

Note to Self: Life is very *good.*

ACKNOWLEDGMENTS

· · · · · · · · · · · ·

SINCERE THANKS TO MY WONDERFUL EDITORS, Emellia Zamani and Anne Shone, who "got" me and my story, and Emily Seife, who continues to champion the *Mission*; my super-agent, Molly Jaffa, who encouraged me every step of the way; my insightful critique partner, Karen Krossing, who asked tough questions during an early draft; and to my family—especially my mom, Kety—and friends for your unwavering support. And finally, love and heartfelt thanks to Rahul, Aftab, and Coby, who continue to inspire me to greater heights with each successive novel.

ABOUT THE AUTHOR

· · · · · · · · · · ·

MAHTAB NARSIMHAN IS THE AUTHOR OF SEVERAL critically acclaimed books, including Silver Birch Award winner *The Third Eye*. Her novel *The Tiffin* was nominated for numerous awards in Canada and was recently published in the United Kingdom and Taiwan. *Mission Mumbai* is her publishing debut in the United States. Mahtab is a native of Mumbai, India, and lives in Toronto, Canada. Visit her online at www.mahtabnarsimhan.com.